"You're a born fighter, Goddess, and I admire that more than you will ever know," Adam said.

Diana closed her eyes and turned away. She didn't want his admiration. She didn't deserve it. Taking her courage firmly in both hands, she decided to be honest. "I'm just not sure I can fight you anymore," she whispered.

"What?"

She met his astonished gaze. "You confuse me. You make me feel—I don't know what you make me feel, except that my body burns up every time you're around."

"That's a start, but is it enough?"

"I don't know. I've never met anyone as hardheaded as you. If you're willing to take the risk, who am I to stop you?"

"You still could," he told her. "Don't do it for my sake. If you really don't want this, tell me now."

Her lips trembled, but she forced herself to steady them. "Backing off so soon, Yankee? What's the matter, didn't figure I'd call your bluff?"

"I never bluff, Diana. Never."

"Then what are you waiting for?" She drew a ragged breath. "Seduce me. . . ."

WHAT ARE *LOVESWEPT* ROMANCES?

They are stories of true romance and touching emotion. We believe those two very important ingredients are constants in our highly sensual and very believable stories in the *LOVESWEPT* line. Our goal is to give you, the reader, stories of consistently high quality that may sometimes make you laugh, sometimes make you cry, but are always fresh and creative and contain many delightful surprises within their pages.

Most romance fans read an enormous number of books. Those they truly love, they keep. Others may be traded with friends and soon forgotten. We hope that each *LOVESWEPT* romance will be a treasure—a "keeper." We will always try to publish

LOVE STORIES YOU'LL NEVER FORGET
BY AUTHORS YOU'LL ALWAYS REMEMBER

The Editors

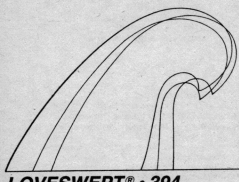

LOVESWEPT® • 394

Courtney Henke
Jinx

BANTAM BOOKS
NEW YORK • TORONTO • LONDON • SYDNEY • AUCKLAND

JINX

A Bantam Book / April 1990

*If you would be interested in receiving protective vinyl
covers for your Loveswept books, please write to this address
for information:*

*Loveswept
Bantam Books
P.O. Box 985
Hicksville, NY 11802*

ISBN 0-553-44032-2

Published simultaneously in the United States and Canada

*Bantam Books are published by Bantam Books, a division
of Bantam Doubleday Dell Publishing Group, Inc. Its trademark, consisting of the words "Bantam Books" and the
portrayal of a rooster, is Registered in U.S. Patent and
Trademark Office and in other countries. Marca Registrada.
Bantam Books, 666 Fifth Avenue, New York, New York 10103.*

PRINTED IN THE UNITED STATES OF AMERICA

OPM   0 9 8 7 6 5 4 3 2 1

To Kurt—

For the lifetime before and the lifetime yet to come. Thank you for sharing it with me, beloved.

Prologue

Adam Daniels strode through the office door, halting abruptly when he saw the petite woman raise her pistol. "Don't—"

Something flew past his ear with a whisper of cold air and landed with a *thwick*. Indignant, Adam glanced at the rubber-tipped dart still quivering beside him, then back to the woman seated behind the cluttered desk. "Hey, watch the coif!" He fluffed his shaggy black hair with an air of hauteur, his blue eyes twinkling. "Mr. David worked hours to achieve this casually rumpled effect."

"And well worth the effort," Emma Machlen Morgan added, reloading quickly. "Stubborn, pig-headed—" She licked the suction tip and aimed carefully, spitting out the next word with loathing. "Sister!" The dart found its target. Without pause, she reached for another. "Is Max with you?" She reloaded again, her expression determined.

"Your husband's over in the—Emma, will you

put that thing down!" He straightened and stood between her and her objective. "What's going on?"

"Don't worry about it, Adam. Diana's just bein' her typical, irrational self." Emma brushed her brown hair from her brow, and her gaze sharpened. "Now, get out of my way, or you'll look like a dimestore unicorn."

Adam folded his arms. He'd seen that look before, the day she had decided Max was the man for her, and it meant trouble for her target. When Emma had blown into his best friend's life the previous summer, determined to sell Max her family's perfume, the little hurricane had shattered Max's protective shell, something Adam had been attempting ever since Max had been blinded in an accident just three months after Adam had begun working for him. Adam had watched in glee while she'd done her job so thoroughly that Max had fallen in love with her.

But this time Adam wanted to protect. He glanced behind him to the framed pastel rendering that had helped create the hottest perfume in the history of the industry. He stared at the stunning woman who had haunted his dreams for months. Though his gaze softened, his voice throbbed with drama. "Ah, yes, the beauteous Diana, goddess of the night, defender of the faith, keeper of the—" Something hit the back of his head. He turned to his friend with a wry tilt of his chin. "Thanks a lot."

Emma grinned unrepentantly. "I warned you." Reluctantly, she put the pistol down. "Are you leaving now?"

"Just about. Got on my lucky jeans, and my baby's gassed up and rarin' to hit the road. I'll send for the rest of my stuff when I get settled."

"Have you finally decided where you're headed?"

"Chicago, I guess. There's a great PR firm that wanted to meet with me. Or maybe New York—I had four offers there." He shrugged. "I'll land on my feet somewhere."

"Of course you will. You're the best people person I know. But we want you to stay. Daniels Cosmetics should have been yours in the first place."

He grimaced. "Only according to my so-called family, Little Bit. My adoptive parents felt I was next in line, but my grandfather felt differently. He saw great potential in his grandnephew, Max. And at the time, baseball was my real love. Max inherited and he deserved to. I only stuck around this long because Max needed the legs, and the eyes. You're more than that, and you know it. You share the same dream."

Her head tilted. "And you have none of your own?"

Adam affected mock surprise. "So serious! I prefer to let life happen to me, instead of the other way around. It's more fun that way." He wriggled his brows. "Besides, thanks to Max, everybody is under the mistaken impression that I know what I'm doing. It's great!"

One corner of her mouth dimpled. "You're an unscrupulous rascal, Adam."

He held up one finger. "I'm immoral, not unscrupulous. There's a difference." After giving Emma an elaborate wink, he gently pried the first dart off the glass over Diana's lush, unbound red hair, tenderly wiping the faint circular mark away with his thumb. He pulled another off with a pop, and his touch lingered on her bare shoulder. "So, your sister's done something horrible, huh?" he murmured, unable to tear his gaze from the portrait. The lids of her half-closed eyes seemed to tremble with longing, her wistful expression communicating her aching need for the phantom embraces of the seven fantasy lovers surrounding her. It always made his breath catch. Adam knew what it was like to yearn for the impossible.

Quickly, before Emma suspected any deeper emotion, he cleared his throat and reached for the dart over the fragile red rosebud that brushed Diana's cheek in an absent caress. He turned to Emma with wide, innocent eyes. "What'd the witch do?"

His barb worked, as he'd expected. "Hey, nobody talks like that about my sister but me! You've never even met her." She huffed and pinched her lids shut. "That *witch* is about to ruin this company, that's what. Max sweat blood to get this place back on its feet, and now, just when we're showing the biggest profit in history, Diana refuses to give up one of her damnable journals!" She reached for her pistol.

Adam leapt for her and wrestled it out of her hand. "Calm down, Little Bit, or I'll kiss you full on the mouth." He sighed mournfully. "Then, unable to resist me, of course, you'd be forced to leave Max heartbroken."

When she didn't smile, Adam became honestly concerned. Though he had burned his bridges with the company, Emma and Max were his friends, and they'd never excluded him from their problems or their joy. At least, they never had before.

Batting the pistol from hand to hand, he said, "Why don't you tell Uncle Adam all about it? I thought Diana was off somewhere researching some obscure medicinal plant or something." It was one of the few things he knew about her. "Your friend Cissy is the only one who knows where she is, and you haven't seen Diana or talked to her in over a year."

Emma snorted. "Yeah, well, I talked to her this morning, for all the good it did me. We Machlens are obsessive about our privacy, but I'm telling you, she makes the rest of us look like publicity hounds!" She thumped the desk with her fists. "I could just kill her! You know the perfume was my mother's, right? Well, the fixative, the barometer grass essence, was discovered by Diana years ago. Only the three of us Machlens know the entire rendering process, and it's the key to our perfume. Dammit, it's the biggest thing to hit the entire industry! And it's worth millions to both my family and to Max's company, *because it's a secret*." Her eyes narrowed in disgust on the portrait. "Yesterday, a rival firm approached my mother, offering her a fortune for the process."

His mouth went dry, and the pistol dropped. He owed Max more than he could ever repay, and if word had finally leaked out . . . "But she refused, right? Max has exclusive rights to it!" Realization dawned. "Diana has a written copy and won't even give it to you for safekeeping? But that's—"

"Irrational, mule-headed, and stubborn?" Emma nodded and held out her hand. "Give me back my gun."

Ignoring her request, Adam let his gaze fly to the wall. He couldn't believe the gentle woman of the portrait would be so unreasonable, and it twisted his heart. "Can't you talk to her again?"

"I'm planning on it, but I don't know how much good it'll do." Emma picked up a piece of paper from the desk. "I finagled the most complicated directions I've ever seen out of Cissy, to Diana's cabin. She's in the Ozarks, of all places! Practically in our backyard!" Emma sighed and let the map flutter away, sinking her head to her hands. "This is killing me, Adam. I respect my sister's privacy, but, dammit, if they know about Mama, how long before they find Diana too? The pharaoh had locusts, we have industrial spies! You know they'll just steal her journal!"

Inspiration flared like a beacon in Adam's mind. "Not if I get there first," he muttered under his breath, and surreptitiously edged the map toward himself. . . .

One

A lover's kiss is coming soon.

Diana stared blankly at the ring her coffee grounds had formed in the bottom of her cup, a shiver running up her spine as the Ozark superstition echoed through her mind.

A lover's kiss is coming soon.

"Nonsense," she whispered. "It's a dirty cup." Besides, she knew that no lover would enter her life ever again. No man was that brave or that stupid, and it had nothing to do with some quirk of fate. It was simply the truth.

Movement flickered at the edge of her vision, thankfully distracting her from the disturbing omen. The lowering sun sent pillars of shadow throughout the rustic room, but she hardly noticed. Her eyes narrowed on a tiny black cat with his nose in her bowl. He glanced up inquiringly.

"Ack," he said, his whiskers quivering.

"I'm immune to charm, and you know it, you clown."

Apparently, he did, for with only a momentary

hesitation, he snatched a morsel and leapt to the floor.

She slammed her cup to the table. "I'm goin' to make a pot holder out of you!" she cried as she lunged, but the tip of his broken tail eluded her as he zoomed around the cabin. "Why can't you be like every other cat in the universe and just *glare* at me when you want food!" She darted toward him and tripped over the edge of a colorful throw rug, sprawling with a surprised *woooof* of expelled breath.

Before she could recover, he banked off the horse-hair sofa and vaulted onto her head, worrying bright red strands out of her French braid with his paws. Then he sprang away, and Diana was left grabbing empty air and tendrils of her hair. He zigzagged between the potted bay laurel and the purple basil, twisting midair to avoid a lamp.

"Dodger, you mangy runt!"

When he headed toward her shotgun, she scrambled up, but he quickly changed direction and bolted toward the bathroom.

He could wriggle through that broken window faster than spit, she knew, and she'd spend all evening coaxing him from beneath the porch. "Shoot!" she muttered, and thumped the smooth wall.

After forcing his precious red Porsche over a rutty path one could only laughingly call a road, Adam found that the sight of the rustic cabin lifted his spirits considerably. Several smooth-planked extensions had been added on to the structure, nearly obscuring the original log cabin. Two chimneys stood at either end like sentinels, one curling smoke. After a quick glance at the map, he nodded and grinned. "Target zero," he muttered, then exited his car and strode through the circular clearing toward the house.

A small window stood ajar just to one side of the porch, and as he passed beneath it, he racked his brain for an excuse to be there, as he had during his entire drive. How could he allay Diana's suspicions? And what would he do if Diana truly was a gentle goddess who could bewitch his soul?

"Dodger, get back here!" shrieked a feminine voice.

From out of nowhere, a tiny black form attached itself to his face. Adam bellowed in outrage and pain as hundreds of little needles pierced his cheeks and his scalp. He grappled with his attacker and flung it from him. It streaked under the porch.

"You scared him, damn you!"

A tall, frizzy-haired apparition wearing an orange sweater and jeans bore down on him. His heart jumped into his throat, and he cried out again. The apparition pointed a long finger at him, and he leapt backward. "You scared my cat!" she said, then turned and bent to scramble after the animal.

Stunned, Adam Daniels could only stare at her, her shapely fanny failing to raise one iota of appreciation. "It's even worse than I thought," he muttered.

She stiffened at the sound of his voice, then scuttled out from under the porch. Her hair, the color of bittersweet and nearly as bright as her sweater, obscured most of her face. But he could see her tilted eyes. Numbly, he continued to stare. "Your eyes," he whispered in shock.

"What?"

He swallowed convulsively. "Dear Lord, your eyes!" A shudder of pleasure rippled through him. Her eyes were a color he'd heard of but never believed existed, the color of a summer sky at dusk. "You have violet eyes." Every inch of skin he possessed tightened with painful intensity. Behind her shock, he sensed the same wistful yearning that had captured his imagination. "Oh, Goddess, do you know how often I've dreamed of those eyes? Ever since I saw your picture, I've fantasized . . ."

For an instant, Diana stood frozen, mesmerized by the stranger's husky voice. The lowering sun lighted his shaggy hair, burnishing it like a raven's wing. Clear features and lean masculinity combined in a potent mixture, the tiny scratches lacing his cheek giving him a rakish air. The beginnings of a slightly naughty smile touched his full mouth, and Diana swallowed hard. He had the same wicked allure of a chocolate fudge cake, and like everything else she knew was bad for her, he called to her baser instincts.

Canadian tundra, she thought frantically, fighting his allure the only way she knew how by thinking of the coldest place she could imagine.

"Dodger," she said in a low tone, feeling behind her for the rail. Then she made an odd sound with her lips.

Ten sharp, needlelike claws pierced Adam's jeans, his yowl shattering the charged air between them. He glared at the tiny cat that hugged his calf as if it were a giant mouse. Adam caught the animal at the scruff of its neck, and gently but firmly peeled it away from his jeans. Then, cradling the growling monster in his palms while it chewed on his thumb, he jerked his head up.

The cold gray twin barrels of a shotgun stared back at him.

"Put the cat down, Yankee."

"This is a cat? I thought it was an inkblot." He deposited the furry bundle carefully on the ground, and it streaked past her through the open cabin door. He rubbed his abused thumb and dabbed at his cheek. The lengths he'd go to for a friend! he thought.

"Now." Her hands firmed on the butt of the gun. "Who are you?"

He crossed his arms over his chest, his mind working quickly. "Adam Daniels."

Oops, he thought as she stiffened, strike one.

"I know that name, Yankee. You're a friend of Emma's, and you work with her. You've come for that damned journal, haven't you?"

"I'll bet you took the gold medal in the conclusion jump," he muttered.

Her violet eyes narrowed. "Well, you can tell her from me—"

"Emma?" He forced a puzzled frown to his brow. "The names sounds vaguely familiar, but . . ."

Her cool gaze never wavered. "Don't try and con me, Yankee."

"*Moi*?" Cocking his head, he eyed her intently. It was as if someone had blown up a Diana Machlen balloon with arctic air, chilling any foolish hope he might still have that she was his goddess. This was a woman who wouldn't allow herself the kind of vulnerability that stupid artist had given her. It must have been a joke, he thought, but he refused to allow it to be on him.

He shivered dramatically. "I left my coat in the car, and I'm freezing out here, Goddess. And my face stings from the damage *your* cat did. Why don't we go in and discuss this in front of a fire?"

The barrel rose fractionally. "I think we're just fine here."

He raised his brows. "I saw a rose once, after it had been dipped in liquid nitrogen." He smiled. "Will you shatter if I touch you too?"

Her eyes narrowed. "Tell me about the journals, and what picture of me have you seen? And don't lie to me, or I'll scatter your innards all over the county."

Strike two, he thought, then grinned as inspiration struck. "All right, Goddess, I'll admit I, er, prevaricated about Emma. But it's only because she never talks about you, and I thought that maybe there was some bad blood between you."

When Diana didn't shoot him, he went on, "But you're Emma's sister. And as long as I worked with her, you were strictly off-limits. But I recently resigned, and finding myself between jobs, with time on my hands . . ." He flashed her his best smile. "Well, to be honest, I saw your portrait, and I knew I had to meet you someday. The opportunity finally arose, and I never question fate. I think you're the most beautiful woman I've ever seen," he said simply, his voice lowering to a purr. "And I've wanted you for months." That was gospel.

"So you're an out-of-work lunatic who's seen some woman in a *picture* and has become obsessed with her?"

He grimaced. It did sound pretty bad. "More or less."

Anger lighted her violet eyes with flames of sapphire. "If you're tryin' to frighten me, trust me—don't."

"I don't frighten women," he said solemnly. "I seduce them."

"In a pig's eye, Yankee," she growled, obviously fighting her temper.

Great, he thought. Strike three. If he wasn't

careful, his body would soon be filled with tiny little holes. And he hadn't even kissed her yet!

That he still wanted to didn't entirely surprise him. "You are lovely, you know that? A goddess of fire and ice."

"As long as we're getting elemental," she said with a brittle smile, "I suppose you're a big bag of wind."

Adam chuckled. Oh yes, this might turn out to be fun after all. And in many ways, her antagonism made it easier. He would wriggle his way into her house, using his besottedness as an excuse, somehow find the book, and then disappear. Only a small part of him wept, and he hurriedly hushed his screaming conscience. He owed Max too much.

Instinct took him forward. "I don't talk when I can act."

"Stop!"

"You are so sexy when you're angry."

"I said stop, Yankee!" She tightened her finger on the trigger.

He flashed her a dazzling smile. "Goddess, you won't shoot me."

Without blinking, she lowered the barrel and pulled the trigger. Sound blasted his eardrums, and dirt splattered his jeans as it erupted from the ground before him. His smile froze, but he didn't flinch. "Correct your sights next time, please. I've always thought ventilated running shoes would be more comfortable."

Diana pumped the gun and raised it again. "If I had aimed at your shoes, I would have hit them." After an eternal pause, she lowered her shotgun and set it against the railing, still well within her reach. "You can tell Emma that I protect what's mine."

He bowed gallantly, his gaze holding hers. "You give the word new meaning, Goddess."

One corner of her mouth tilted wryly, giving her triangular face a feral look. "You don't know the half of it, Yankee. Remember that next time you try and con me." She dropped her gaze and shivered. "Not that I actually believe you about the picture, but I guess I should attend to those scratches." She lifted her gaze. "But don't get any ideas. I find you infinitely resistible."

Knowing he had to get into her cabin to find the journals, and suspecting she'd bandage him on the porch, he bowed again. "Why, thank you, I'd love to see your home." Ignoring her startled exclamation, Adam pushed past her into the cabin. He halted in the doorway, glancing around. The furniture, solid and practical and built with no eye to beauty, stood grouped precisely, delineated not by walls but by bright rugs lying diagonally between items. Gleaming appliances lined the kitchen area, and three doors led out of the main room. Everywhere, splashes of color and lush, potted plants met his eye, creating a snug warmth at complete odds with her icy personality.

The cat lifted its muzzle from a bowl on the sturdy table, hissed, and leapt for him again. It bit his ankle, then bounded away.

Adam glared at it and decided to ignore it. "This isn't what I expected," he murmured, sniffing at a luscious food odor.

"Oh, we're quite modern, Slick. We paneled the outhouse last Thursday. Not that it's any business of yours, but judging by your car, I could live for a year on what you make—made—in a week. I'm a very practical person." Diana watched in amazement as her unwelcome intruder strode to the stove and took a bite of her dinner. She must have imagined his flash of humanity. "Help your-self," she said with a touch of sarcasm. Her jaw dropped when he did, then seated himself. "Are you this obnoxious naturally, or do you have to work at it?"

He grinned. "It's a gift." He indicated his bowl. "Hey, this is fantastic! What is it?"

Her eyes narrowed. "Snake."

He paused with the spoon raised halfway to his mouth, and a ludicrous expression of dismay crossed his face. "You're kidding."

Pressing her lips tightly together, she nodded. "Of course." She paused. "It's squirrel."

"Right," he said, and took another bite.

Not for anything in the world would she tell him she'd told the truth about the squirrel, she thought. But what did he truly want? One minute he scorched her with blatant promise in his eyes, the next he shoved his way into her house as if he owned it. He had violated her privacy, and though it angered her, she was grateful. She had the feeling that when he wanted to, Adam Daniels could seduce a woman as easily as he thought he could.

Her smile was grim. She could almost hope for the disaster that would befall him if he succeeded with her. He deserved whatever he got.

"How's your insurance?" she asked sweetly.

"Is this a test?"

Quickly, Diana sat next to him. Dodger must be hiding beneath the sofa, she thought, otherwise this smug Yankee would be wearing his stew. She almost called her pesky cat out but decided enough time had been wasted. "All right, Adam Daniels. Why don't you tell me why you're really here."

He dropped his spoon and rocked back in the chair. "I told you. I saw your portrait and—"

She waved that away. "I've never even heard of any portrait of me, and even if it did exist, I wouldn't believe it brought you here."

"Your niece Catherine used your exquisite face as a model for the most erotic advertising campaign I've ever seen. Emma used it to sell Max the perfume your family developed."

Diana's conviction wavered. Catherine *was* an artist, and it would be just like Emma to depict the family iceberg. "Was I at least clothed?" she asked acidly.

"Fully," he told her, his blue eyes twinkling. "But it didn't hide your . . . assets."

Diana turned away, forcing the image of an arctic wasteland into her mind. Despite his cocksure attitude, Adam Daniels was quite appealing.

"You honestly don't know you're a legend in the industry, do you?"

She smiled wryly. "I've found that there's usually a core of scientific truth in legends, Yankee. But—"

Before she could finish the thought, she felt her cold hand pressed between two warm ones. Startled, she glanced at Adam, who gazed at her with the blatant sexuality she'd tried to ignore.

"I'm very happy to finally meet you, Diana Machlen." Slowly, he raised her hand to his mouth.

Electricity shot through her at the touch of his lips on her fingers. "But not in this case," she said, and couldn't remember why.

His voice lowered to a husky rumble as he turned it over and pressed another kiss into her palm. "You feel it too, don't you?" he murmured. "We sizzle, Goddess."

"So does a drop of water on a griddle," she said dazedly. "Then it just . . . evaporates."

"I want to know you better. Much better."

She jerked her hand back, thinking *Aspen ski slopes.* It didn't work.

A keening growl filled the cabin. Oh, no! she thought.

"What's that?" he asked.

"Dodger," she said, glancing around. She *knew* something would happen if she let this situation get out of control!

"Is he going to explode?"

The sound grew louder. "No. You'd better tense up."

"What?"

"Dammit, tense up! And get—"

Before she could complete her warning, a streak of black fur came out of nowhere, then bounded off the table and onto his chest. Adam went tumbling backward with a crash.

"Are you all right?" Concerned, she knelt beside him.

He snatched her arm and pulled her on top of him. "You have the most interesting household," he muttered.

His breath warmed her cheek, his hard body seemed to ignite hers. But Dodger, zooming around the cabin behind her, kept her turbulent emotions at bay. She rolled off swiftly and glared down at Adam. "Cut that out!"

He sprang to his feet with the grace and fluidity of a predatory beast. "I knew the earth would move with you."

"That wasn't me, it was that execrable cat!" Warily, she watched Dodger, not Adam, and that was her mistake.

"That remains to be seen," he murmured, and strode through the door, only a slight limp from his fall slowing him. "I'll get my overnight bag."

"Wait!" His audacity made her gasp. She scrambled after him, pausing at the jamb. "What are you talking about?"

"It's too late to drive back to St. Louis before dark!" he cried over his shoulder as he ran toward his car. His arms waved wide. "You wouldn't be so cruel as to deny me a place to sleep after all you've put me through!"

"You can't stay!" she shouted. "I only have one bed!"

"Okay by me!" he called happily.

The image of Adam intertwined with her on her big featherbed finally broke the frantic hold she had on her emotions. "No!" she cried. Dodger darted past her and banked off the shotgun. It toppled and fell.

The world around her exploded.

Her heart thumping madly, Diana risked a quick, horrified glance into the clearing. He was still standing, ramrod-stiff, next to the red sportscar. Oh, thank the Lord, Adam was alive and in one piece. Relief flooded her, and she started toward him.

His bellow brought her up short.

His eyes narrowed. "I knew something would happen. I knew you were too perfect." His gaze raked her thoroughly, with no trace of his earlier lust. "I just knew something would go wrong."

He stepped backward, winced, and glanced around behind him. He closed his eyes tightly, nodding as if he'd expected it. "I'm bleeding."

Two

"You shot me!"

Several holes marked his left jeans pocket, and an ominous stain was spreading. "You're—" The blood left Diana's face in a rush, leaving her reeling. "I didn't shoot—" She swallowed hard. She hadn't pulled the trigger, but it *had* been her fault. "It was an accident, Adam. Dodger hit the gun, and it fell. C'mon, we have to see how bad it is."

He obviously wasn't listening. "Of course," he said, as if it were the most natural thing on earth for him to be standing in the middle of the road, bleeding all over himself. "Of course you shot me. I forgot—just for a moment, mind you—that you're not who I thought you were." He nodded and eyed her appraisingly. "This is what always happens when I fantasize, did you know that?"

There was a green tinge around his mouth, and his blue eyes were glazed. Shock, she thought, biting back an acid retort. She took his arm, galvanized into action. "I have to get you to a hospital," she said, then stopped with uncharacteristic indecision. The nearest one was almost an hour away. Shuddering, she realized she'd have to do this herself, and drew on her inherent practicality. "C'mon. I have to get you to the cabin."

"Why? To finish the job? Why don't you just plunge a knife through my heart and get it over with?"

She ignored his outburst and dragged him. "I have to see how bad it is, and take out any buckshot."

He stopped suddenly. "Do you realize," he said, "that if I'd turned the other way, you would have made Swiss cheese out of the family jewels?"

Remorse flooded her, but she forced herself to be strong. "Adam, please stop talking and hurry."

He limped beside her, frowning in puzzlement. "It doesn't hurt. It's just numb." He shook his head and gave her a ghost of his earlier jaunty smile. "Nice shot."

"Just shut up and walk, Yankee," she said with a growl.

With her slender, determined form setting the pace, Adam hobbled quickly into the cabin and through the main room. Diana deposited him facedown on a neatly made bed, then hurried away to gather what she would need. While she was gone, Adam berated himself for losing all of his famous aplomb. Good grief, he'd practically fainted like some Victorian maiden!

Propping himself up on one elbow, he gazed down the length of his leg, touching the bloodied spots gingerly. He felt little twinges of pain, and he sighed in relief. The shock had just numbed his system, he decided; it wasn't nerve damage.

A self-mocking smile curved his mouth as he sank his head back to the frilly pillow, his arms curled beneath it. Well, he thought with a snort, this was exactly where he'd wanted to be, in her bed. He'd made it, all right, but as usual it wasn't exactly the way he'd planned it. This was downright embarrassing! Why was it that every time he built something up in his mind, every time he wanted something so badly he could taste it, it all fell apart? His baseball career had been a nightmare, his family life a joke, and now his goddess had turned out to be a homicidal maniac!

He frowned, remembering her denial, and realized it had to be true. He had a suspicion that anything she aimed at she hit. But, dammit, that just made it worse! Now, because of sheer bad luck, he was incapacitated!

"Then again," he murmured with a grin, "I'm stuck here for a while."

Breathing deeply, he inhaled her scent, left behind on the linens, and something twisted in the region of his heart. Spicy and sweet, he thought, like cloves with a touch of honey. It was exactly like her. One minute she was a pillar of strength, fury, and fire, the next drawing him into the depths of her violet eyes with unnamed delights. She might not be the gentle goddess of his dreams, but she intrigued him more than any other woman he'd ever known.

Arousal tingled through him. He wanted to explore the pleasures of that pale, creamy body. He wanted to feel the fire she tried to deny. The circumstances could have been better, but he'd find a way around them. His quirky luck never failed him; it just threw him a nasty curve once in a while. He would have the journals and his ice maiden, no matter what protests came from her delicious little mouth. Those eyes didn't lie.

Of course, his first action would be to break that damned gun.

She returned quickly, carrying a steaming pan, several towels, a bottle of rubbing alcohol, and a pair of tongs in the crook of her arm. She placed everything on the table beside him, then carefully sat on the edge of the bed, touching his leg gently with a trembling hand. "Looks like about seven pieces." Her voice quivered. "They're not too deep—you just caught the edge of the pattern—but I'll have to get 'em out before the lead poisons you."

"That's a comforting thought," he murmured, wondering at her obvious concern. She had some warmth beneath that ice, it seemed. But was she worried about him, or about her abilities?

Maybe it was time for a little well-aimed venom. "Where's the Tasmanian devil?"

"Dodger? I locked him in the stillroom."

"Thank heaven," he said heartily.

She paused. "How do you feel?"

He grinned and shot her a smoldering look over his shoulder. "With my fingers."

She gasped and stood abruptly. "Don't you ever think of anything but sex?"

He pondered it for a moment. "Nope."

She growled in frustration and snatched the tongs, using them to lift something from the water while she muttered to herself. "Self-indulgent, self-centered, egotistical, chauvinistic—" she glared at him and spat the last word—"playboy!"

"I'm not a chauvinist!" he protested. "I supported the ERA."

Her delicate nostrils flared, and she shook the tongs at him, spraying water all over his shirt. "I didn't shoot you before, but I will! Right in the mouth, Yankee!"

He wriggled his eyebrows. "I knew it! You love me!"

"Oh!" Chest heaving, Diana spun away from

him. "This is going to give me great pleasure," she muttered through clenched teeth.

When she turned, brandishing scissors, Adam suffered a slight qualm. "What are you doing?"

One corner of her mouth lifted wickedly. "I'm going to dig that shot out of your wretched backside. But first . . ." She tucked the blade beneath his hem. "I'm going to cut your pants off."

"No! Wait!" He reached beneath him and unsnapped, then unzipped himself. "Have a heart. These are my lucky jeans!"

"Some luck," she muttered, but withdrew the shears. "It'll hurt that way," she said sweetly.

"Won't you love that." Slowly, he slid his jeans over his briefs, then, gritting his teeth, over his legs. She was right. It did hurt. But he wouldn't give her the pleasure of knowing it, especially since she'd finally stopped shaking. "You'll have to pull them off," he told her when he could reach no farther.

Her eyebrows raised when she saw his underwear. "Zebra stripes?"

"They were a gift."

"I see." Diana stifled her laughter and pulled his jeans off. She didn't want to laugh, dammit! She wanted to kill him!

No, she admitted when she studied his half-naked form, she didn't want to kill him. His firm buttocks, outlined beneath the black-and-white pattern, made her breathing ragged, made her tighten her grip convulsively on the denim, made her dream impossible dreams. She didn't want to kill him at all. She wanted to—

"Enjoying the view?" he asked.

Frozen yogurt. Flushing, she tossed his pants aside, cursing her wayward body. Even if she could do what her imagination was urging her to do, she wouldn't choose this unstable, flippant Yankee to do it with! She clutched the scissors and slid them under the tiny elastic band of his briefs. "The zebras are dead meat," she said, defying him to stop her.

He shrugged, his gaze turning to fix on a point on the oak headboard. "I don't think Simone would care," he told her. "She never reacted to a simple kiss like you did."

Simone! A woman named Simone had given him this scandalous piece of nylon. She took great pleasure in slicing through it before she glanced up to find his amused gaze on her again. Her eyes narrowed. "That was repulsion, Yankee."

"It was desire, Diana." He cocked his head. "Why do you deny it, I wonder?"

Her lips firmed stubbornly. Her and her big mouth! Now, she'd challenged his ego. "There's nothing to deny."

"Isn't there?" Wincing in pain, he reached over. He placed a finger beneath her chin and tilted her face up. His blue eyes searched hers, confusion creasing his brow. "You wanted me as much as I wanted you, Diana. What's wrong with a little honest emotion?"

Warmth flooded her, but she couldn't allow this to go any further. He couldn't possibly know how much danger he was in at this moment!

Ice caverns. She jerked away from him and dropped her gaze, studying the pattern on her quilt. "That's not emotion, it's chemistry." Her gaze moved upward, over the strong muscles of his legs, his skin sprinkled with dark hairs. Her chest tightened. "It's a body's reaction to"—she swallowed heavily when she reached his firm thighs—"to a basic need."

He chuckled. "I think you've been neglecting a few basic needs for a long time."

"That's none of your business," she told him, denying her body's responses with an effort as she turned away. "Come on, Diana," she murmured. "Get it together."

Taking a deep, cleansing breath, she returned the scissors to the table and dug the forceps out of the water, dousing them liberally with alcohol. It splashed to the floor, and she cursed. What was wrong with her?

"Hey, Goddess, don't worry. Seven is my lucky number."

It figures, she thought, but his words gave her the burst of irritation she needed to pull the rest of her frazzled nerves together. "Just lie down and be quiet, Adam."

"One more question."

She sighed. "What?"

"Have you ever done this before?"

"Sure." She went to him, her mouth lifted wryly. "On a cow."

He half rose. "Wha-at?"

Diana shoved him back. "This'll hurt me more than it'll hurt you, Yankee."

"You don't know how much I wish that were true," he muttered.

The sun was setting by the time she finished her job, but Diana hardly noticed. After she washed her instruments and her hands, she leaned against the perpetually leaky porcelain sink, swallowing a shaky laugh. Lord, she'd done it, but that last piece . . .

With the memory, reaction set in with a vengeance. She'd never purposely caused pain to another human being in her life, and though Adam had kept up a running monologue on her redoubtable virtues, she could tell by his strained tones and all too frequent pauses that her digging was not the high point of his visit. But despite his outrageous behavior, something flushed to life inside of her. Admiration. Adam Daniels might be an out-of-work bum and an opportunistic octopus, but he was not a coward, unlike some people she knew. Not once had that flippant Yankee complained or acted as if they were engaging in anything but an ordinary seduction. For the first time in a long time, she wished it could happen, that she could give in to him and the lure of his wicked blue eyes.

Clearing her throat, she placed all the instruments carefully in their respective places in the bathroom and kitchen, then put the kettle on the stove and went to gather a spoonful of fragrant herbs from the stillroom. When she opened the door, Dodger sat stiffly just over the jamb. He accused her with a glare, damning her to pet-owner hell for his incarceration, then regally swept past her, his broken tail a quivering banner of indignation. She smiled at him, silently thanking heaven for her eccentric roommate. He could always help her regain her treasured balance.

By the time she returned to the bedroom, a hot mug cradled in her palms, her stomach no longer fluttered wildly, and her heartbeat had slowed to almost normal. By no indication would Adam ever know how much he'd affected her. She had the feeling that one word, one tiny look, would be all it would take to make him determined to stay until he had made his conquest. And that could only spell disaster for both of them.

With that in mind, she placed the tea on the table beside him and with a brisk, impersonal nod tugged the sheet up to the fringe of black hair at the base of his neck. He turned his face on the pillow and stared first at her, then at the cup. "Going to finish the job with a little hemlock toddy?"

"Tempting, but no. Just something to ease the pain, and help you sleep. Otherwise, you'll toss and turn all night."

"If you keep me company, I swear I won't bleed all over your sheets."

She sat on the edge of the bed and touched his forehead. "I'll take my lumpy couch, thank you."

"I'm much more comfortable. My lumps are in all the right places."

"Mmm," she murmured distractedly, frowning over his warmth.

"Will I die, Doctor?" he asked with a dramatic quiver.

Concerned, she asked, "Do you feel hot?"

"Yes." He sighed. "All over."

The skin around his mouth was drawn and white, but his blue eyes were clear and—

She pursed her lips. They were clear, all right—clearly looking at her breasts. With a huff, she jerked her hand back and reached into her pocket. "I think you'll survive. But you'll be stiff in the morning."

"I'm st—"

She cut him off midword by shoving a fat red-and-white object into his mouth. He pulled it out and blinked at it. "What in the name of heaven is that?"

"A dipstick." She smiled sweetly. "It'll show how shallow you are." When he still eyed it suspiciously, she huffed. "It's a thermometer, Adam."

"You're going to take my temperature with a candy cane?"

"It's European. I use it to test alcohol baths."

"How do I know where it's been?"

She pried open his mouth and stuck it beneath his tongue. "Trust me."

He grinned around it. "I can think of better things to put there."

"Shhh." After a few minutes of blessed silence, after checking his strong, steady pulse, she withdrew the thermometer and sighed in relief. "You're normal."

"Thanks a lot!"

Diana ignored him and put the cooled cup to his lips, knowing it would act quickly. Some of the tea dribbled over his cheek onto the pillow, drawing her gaze to a faint, ragged etching beside his mouth. "Where did you get that scar?"

"My sister threw a rock. Long story. Where did you get your medical degree?"

Remembering her vow of impersonality, she pulled the mug back, counting mentally. It shouldn't be long, she thought, as he blinked in slow motion. She began to stroke his hair and talk soothingly. Above all else, Adam needed rest now. "Oh, you learn a few things researching medicinal herbs. I sort of inherited this house from the local healer when she passed away three years ago."

"You didn't even tell your own family."

His gently rebuking tone twinged her guilt, forcing her to explain. "Machlens understand privacy better than anybody, Adam. Heck, I have a cousin who's been gone for five years, and there's so many of us, you hardly notice anyone's missing. And this lady and her world were my secret refuge, I guess. She was great. Everyone called her Nana, as if she were grandmother to the universe. She was the most serene woman I've ever known. I met her during a college project, and she welcomed me with open arms. I had the interest her daughter never had."

"You miss her."

Diana smiled crookedly, her eyes suddenly misty. "Yeah, I do." She cleared her throat. "Her will gave me a lease on the cabin for as long as I want it, for a dollar a year. Though no one else has her inclination for herbal healing, her ancestors carved their place in this land, and she didn't want it to pass out of the family's hands. The past was as important to her as the future, intertwined in a way I'm only beginning to realize."

Adam snorted sleepily. "Live for the present," he murmured.

Diana sighed. He *would* feel that way. She pulled her hand back. "Nana kept meticulous records, and her potions will keep me busy for the rest of my life. She taught me everything I know. Including how to stifle temperamental patients."

Adam chuckled, giving in to the lethargy creeping over him. "Now that makes me feel better." When she stood to leave, his hand snaked from beneath the covers and took hers. "Diana, wait." She sat, and Adam swallowed heavily, fighting a wave of dizziness that had suddenly hit him. What had that horrible-tasting stuff been? "I—I have to know something." Embarrassed, he gulped once more. "The shot. It was an accident, wasn't it?"

"Yes." She stood again.

"Wait!" Great, he thought, now he'd insulted her. He didn't want her to hate him, not when he wanted to make magic in her arms! "I didn't mean it like that. I meant that I know it was. You couldn't . . ." He fought to focus, but her beautiful face zigzagged sideways and upside down and then disappeared completely, and he couldn't remember why. But he needed to tell her something, to explain a very important fact. "I'm not shallow," he murmured. At least that was what he thought he said. His tongue felt as though it weighed two pounds. "I'm adopted."

He heard her melodious chuckle, and her answer. "Of course, that explains everything!"

"No, I mean . . ." His voice trailed away, and he felt very pleased that he had finally made her laugh, wanting to do more than that. "I'm . . . really not as . . ."

"Don't talk anymore, Adam. Go to sleep."

He had to tell her . . . but the bed felt so warm and so soft and he was sinking and he couldn't remember. . . . "You *did* poison me," he mumbled.

Just before he drifted off, he could have sworn he felt cool lips pressed to his.

The sensation lingered, and he woke with a smile as the gentle tickling continued. Vaguely, he heard an odd, raucous sound, but only a small part of his mind took points off Diana's score for perfection for snoring. He could live with that as long as she was beside him.

A tiny frown creased his brow, the movement somehow stopping the snore. No lithe body warmed the bed next to him, and his left ear burned, as if he had been lying on it for a long time. Why would it do that?

He opened his eyes. A pair of brown ones stared back, practically on his nose. Both sets widened and jerked away from each other.

Adam gasped. Dodger hissed and arched. Neither was amused.

Spitting indignation, the cat bounded away. After a heart-stopping moment, Adam burst into laughter. This house was a zoo! Why did it intrigue him so much?

When he'd calmed down sufficiently, he glanced around the room. Dim light filtered through the window, showing him his overnight bag and folded, clean jeans draped over a chair. Except for that and the absence of the cup, it was the same as the night before. "Diana?" he called, wondering how long he'd slept. "Goddess?"

Only a distant bird and the faint drip-drip of a leaky faucet answered him. Blinking, he stared at the window and realized that no shade covered it, that a faint line of rose tinged the horizon. Good heavens, it was dawn!

He threw back the warm blanket and pushed himself up. Shivering, gritting his teeth against the burning sensation in his backside, he wrapped the sheet loosely around him and hobbled into the cabin's main room, toward the bathroom. When he exited, he glanced over at the sofa, only to find a stack of folded bedding. Puzzled, he looked around but saw no one. The dirt from yesterday's tramping in and out had been cleaned up, the house was neat and tidy. Where was she? Did she have elves to do her work, or had she been up all night?

Dodger sat stiffly on the table beside two closed books. "Ack," he said.

Her journals! Adam glared at the eccentric guard, and the cat leapt down, stropped his claws on the leg of a chair, then bit Adam on the ankles. Adam sighed as Dodger bounded away. "You're a real saint, you know that?"

Adam turned his attention toward the books, squinting to read the cramped handwriting in the first one. He snorted with laughter. "Powdered chicken gizzards as a cure for stomach problems?" he said aloud. Realizing the journal was one of Nana's, he turned to the other. The neat, flowing script could belong only to Diana. Each page meticulously outlined her steps of research. Faint unease niggled at him, and he flipped to the first page. It was dated less than a month before! The formula for the perfume, he remembered, had been discovered years ago. There had to be more books somewhere.

He closed the journal with a snap, wondering where to look first. And where was Diana? Would she burst in on him at any moment?

Adam limped to the kitchen window and leaned on the sink, glancing around the clearing outside for any sign of Diana. He shifted to take the weight off his twinging muscle. Though the sun had not yet topped the trees, its rays reached out to caress the budding branches with soft fire, to warm the burgeoning ground with its kiss. Smiling despite himself, Adam stood mesmerized as the world came alive.

A movement to his left caught his eye. His heart lurched in his chest. From a wiry break of bushes, Diana wandered into sight, twirling the stems of puffy spring flowers in her fingertips, her boots treading softly. Her bright hair, streaming unbound down her jacket, caught the sun's fire and returned it tenfold. Her creamy complexion glowed, like a pale beacon of peace and harmony, as she touched her cheek with one blossom. Adam's throat tightened. It was the same pose as in the portrait, and her mouth, smiling gently and dreamily, begged to be touched by more than the cool spring breeze.

Adam began to move, to join her in her worship of the dawn, but stopped abruptly when he saw her sink down to sit on a stump, looking back toward the brush. Her exquisite profile indicated she was watching for someone, or something. He cocked his head, wondering who or what she was waiting for. Long moments passed, anticipation flowed through him, then he had his answer.

First a tiny rabbit nosed into view, its whiskers trembling, then another followed, and another. All moved slowly, sensing her presence, but none feared her enough to turn and bolt. The trio edged toward Diana, who sat as still as a statue.

From the other side, a large bird edged into sight, then a fluffy brown squirrel, its tail twitching convulsively. Adam's eyes widened as they were joined by a doe and a handful of quail. A raccoon darted in, then away, and he swore he saw the gray snout of a fox poke from behind a tree trunk. Though none of the creatures actually touched her, Adam sensed that they all had come simply to be near this amazing woman.

The rising sun erupted over the horizon, and the birds burst into an ecstatic song, greeting the day. His dream woman smiled with dazzling intensity.

"Oh, Goddess," he whispered, his heart catching.

Then Diana calmly plucked the flower head from its stem and popped it into her mouth, shattering the image.

Three

With a final scattering of sweet clover, Diana plaited her hair, then retrieved her basket from the brush. The wary animals had almost, but not quite, become accustomed to her presence in their domain, and that pleased her. Except for the raccoons. The pair that had taken up residence nearby had long ago decided their abode simply did not provide enough food. One now picked at the livingroom window with nimble claws, crouched on the sill where he'd found a cooling loaf of persimmon bread last week.

"Crockett," she whispered in a commanding tone, knowing that her house would be a shambles if they ever succeeded in their quest for admittance. "Shoo! Go on, you pest, shoo!"

The male bandit darted a quick look her way, then scampered off with his mate.

Diana smiled after them, shaking her head, then drew deep breaths of the fresh, bracing air. In her corner of the Ozarks, the shadow of the bluff that protected her cabin from the full onslaught of winter also delayed the spring, creating a chill that would disappear over the next week as the sun changed its trajectory. But further afield, jonquils, crocuses, and redbud bloomed now; mustard, dandelion, and plantain flourished. Each in its own way was valuable to her—some because of their beauty, some because they filled her stomach.

And some, like the tiny dog violet she carried in her basket, provided her with living research material. "Gathered with the morning dew still upon them," she muttered, repeating Nana's instructions as she walked around the cabin. These would be the final addition she needed for the tonic that had fascinated her all year, the potion that, if she was right, contained the heart accelerator that would be the focus of her latest paper. She hoped that ingredient was the dog violet.

She entered the cabin on silent feet, not willing to disturb her unwelcome patient. His skin had been cool this morning when she'd left, and he needed his sleep so he could heal quickly and leave as soon as possible. At least, that's what she told herself. As she placed her basket beside the kitchen sink, it occurred to her that Adam Daniels had already wriggled into a corner of the heart she had thought fully insulated against men, and that made her uneasy in his presence.

"It's simply that ridiculous injury," she whispered to Dodger as he sniffed the flowers. "But it didn't still that smart-aleck tongue of his." And that had probably protected him, she thought wryly. His comments aggravated her, making it easier to forget his sexuality, and his rakish vulnerability.

"Why can't I experience it just once?" she asked Dodger. "Is it so wrong to want to find out if he's right, if there really is such a thing as magic?"

Dodger mewed, then returned to the flowers.

Diana sighed. "Why am I asking you?"

Dodger, deciding the blossoms were inedible, vaulted off the counter and toward the bedroom. Adam's low voice murmured something, causing her heart to leap almost painfully in her chest. He was awake!

Clearing her throat, she slid into her chair at the table, opening her journal to the proper page. Her normally neat handwriting wobbled a bit, but she forced her hand to still while she entered her morning's findings. There had been a promising burgeoning in the south glade, she remembered, but she had forgotten her camera to record it. If she was right, it was a species of orchid thought extinct in this area. Dutifully, she jotted down the sighting, and racked her brain to find the reason she'd sat down in the first place. The tonic, that was it.

"Good morning."

His voice, husky with sleep, made her jump. "Good morning," she said casually, forcing her hand to keep writing.

The silence following her greeting sounded unnaturally loud. She glanced out of the corner of her eye. Adam stood in the bedroom doorway, dressed in a sheet fashioned toga-style. The top of his dark head nearly brushed the shelves that ran the length of the walls into the kitchen, too high for her to reach unassisted. His broad shoulders seemed even broader in the silly garb, his muscled leanness lending it an air of masculinity that had Diana briefly bemoaning the fall of Rome. "Couldn't get into your own pants, either, huh?" she asked acidly.

"Not over the bandage."

"I'll try to find you something looser," she told him, dragging her reluctant gaze back to her pages.

"Thanks, but I have a pair of sweatpants in the car. If you could—"

"Sure, after breakfast." Taut moments stretched on. Diana stirred in her chair, wondering why he hadn't shot one of his well-aimed barbs her way. Her arctic ice was melting. Come on, Adam, she urged silently, say something hateful! "You shouldn't be out of *my* bed."

"Sorry, I'll sleep on the couch tonight."

Disappointed with his quiet answer, Diana raised her eyes. He hadn't moved. And he was studying her as if he'd never seen her before. "That's not necessary," she said, frowning. "I'm shorter."

He looked away first. "I, uh, couldn't find any toothpaste. I used your baking soda. I hope that was okay."

"It's fine, Adam." Her chest tightened, astonishing her with the realization that this had nothing to do with protection. His newfound indifference *hurt.* "The toothpaste is usually in the little linen closet by the tub, but I'm out anyway."

"Then how come your breath's so—" He cut himself off and tugged the edge of the sheet.

Her breasts hardened as the movement exposed the length of his long leg, but she thought of a snow cone, and the fleeting urge passed. This was so unfair! "Eat the one in the middle, the mossy-looking one," she told him with a nod toward the windowsill. "Better than breath mints."

"Thanks, Snow White, I'll pass."

Diana turned back to her journal. "Your funeral," she said, cursing her foolish pride. That was all it was, she told herself; he'd stung her pride with his attitude, prompting her to provoke him.

Cursing again silently, she stood, dragged two

apples from the refrigerator, and snatched her corer from a drawer. "So, Sleazy, are you hungry?"

"Ooo, low blow, Snow," he said, a quiver of amusement in his voice. "Or did you mean to say Sneezy? Or—who are the rest? Let's see . . . Doc, Grumpy, Happy—"

"Dopey," she put in quickly, grateful for the return of the smart-ass.

"—Sleepy, and . . . I always forget the last one."

"Bashful." She shot him a look over her shoulder and reached for her knife. "It's no wonder you forgot that one."

"It's a wonder I remember any of them at all," he murmured, then crossed his arms over his chest and grinned lopsidedly. "Then again, I even surprise myself sometimes."

"A real red-letter day, that," she told him sweetly, and concentrated on making perfect apple rings, not on how his smile made her feel like cornmeal mush inside. "Are you hungry?"

His smile faded abruptly, and he shifted his body. "What's for breakfast?"

"Braised apples with cinnamon, pumpkin toast, milk, and . . . coffee." Blushing, she reached for the filter, busying herself with the preparation. Every time she thought of coffee, she remembered that stupid omen in the ring in her cup the day before, and it irritated her. Adam Daniels could never become her lover. It was high time she remembered that.

"Don't you have anything but gerbil food?"

She bit back a sharp retort, reminding herself that his injury was indirectly her fault, and that he was still convalescing. Besides, he was safer if she hated his guts. Breathing deeply, she turned. "What would you like?"

He moved to the table. "Eggs and bacon?"

"Your cholesterol count must be astronomical," she muttered, but got out her last two eggs. "Compromise. I'll add these to the menu, but no bacon. How do you like them?"

"Scrambled, please."

She cracked the eggs into a small bowl, added chervil and chives, and grabbed a fork.

"Do powdered chicken gizzards really help your stomach?"

"What?" The sound of paper rustling spun her about. "Hey!" She stomped over to him and slammed her journal shut, nearly catching his fingers in it. "These are mine, Yankee."

He lifted both hands in a gesture of surrender. "I forgot how touchy you Machlens are about your privacy."

"You try growing up with twelve brothers and sisters!"

"And cousins."

"Don't laugh, Yankee. Nobody reads these journals but me. Nobody! My research will get me a Nobel someday. Beneath the mysticism and the superstition lies a solid, practical reason for most cures. Thanks to that particular piece of folk medicine," she snapped, "doctors discovered a drug for the stomach. And thanks to the practice of putting moldy, masticated bread on cuts—"

"Penicillin. I get the picture, Snow. I was just curious."

She brandished her fork. "You and Dodger can stick your curiosity right—"

"Temper, temper." He grinned and sank toward the chair. "Your blood press—" The word ended in a yowl as he abruptly stood, his face contorted.

"What's wrong?"

"Dammit, I can't even sit down!" He huffed and glared at the seat. "This is so embarrassing."

"That's it. Back you go." She took his arm and tugged him toward the bedroom, but he refused to budge and snatched it back. She stamped her foot. "Don't be stubborn, Adam! You shouldn't be walking around yet, and you know it!"

"I'm fine." Gingerly, holding his body rigid, he sat, hanging half of his bottom off the chair. "See?" A fine sheen of perspiration dampened his brow. "I'm a rock."

She frowned in concern. "Maybe I should stay home today."

"Please, I don't want to disrupt your precious research. Nobel Prize, remember? Dodger and I can get along very well, thank you, and I'll be gone before you know it. Now." He cleared his throat, raising his voice. "I'm hungry, woman. Feed me."

Her mouth pursed, but she turned back to the bowl, shooing Dodger away impatiently. What a macho act, she thought. He deserved his pain, for as long as he stayed. It would keep him away from her, and that was exactly what she wanted. She would finish making breakfast, but she refused to feel guilty for leaving him alone for the day. "I don't know when I'll be back," she told him as she whipped the eggs, trying to control her angry inner battle. "But if I'm not home by lunch, there's soup in the refrigerator." Froth splattered her cheeks with the force of her blows. "And I hope you choke on it!"

"That sounds like a curse," he said quietly.

Her hand clenched. "Maybe it was meant to be one."

"You have to watch things like that. Baseball players are a notoriously superstitious breed."

"I thought you worked with my sister's husband."

"Oh, I quit baseball a long time ago."

Something beneath his jaunty tone tugged at

her heart, but she steadfastly refused to soften. "Then you won't mind a little curse, will you?"

He knocked wood with a grin, and she rolled her eyes heavenward.

Adam stared across the room at the closed still-room door for several long minutes, debating with himself. Diana had taken her journals in after breakfast, then slung her shotgun and Polaroid over her shoulder, and returning long enough to throw his sweatpants in his face, she had stomped out without a backward glance. Either she was incredibly trusting or incredibly naive.

He stood slowly, wincing at his backside's stiff protest, and took one hesitant step, then another. His legs trembled with the effort, but he forced himself forward, no matter how his morning's exertions had tired him. This was for Max, he told himself firmly, each reason taking him another foot closer to the door. He owed everything to Max. Max had been the only member of his adoptive family ever to treat him like a human being, the only man to believe in him enough to give him a real job in the family business after his failed baseball career had left him shaking and insecure. If Diana had simply agreed to give Max the journal in the first place, he wouldn't even have considered searching it out. But he had to protect Max, and the company that was his life's blood. And Diana . . .

He paused with his hand on the knob, his inner vision replaying every moment with his flame-haired wildcat. Desire, ferocious and sweet, coursed through him. She was the most spirited, courageous woman he'd ever known. Defying him—and the safe, conventional world—at every turn, Diana caused a fire to burn inside of him. This was something he'd never experienced with any other woman, and it was beginning to worry him. Diana Machlen had destroyed his image of a dreamy-eyed Venus over and over, but every time it happened, his desire for her came back, stronger than before, and he didn't completely understand why. In the past, when his dreams had died, he had only been disillusioned, resentful, even violently angry once. But he had always bounced back, and he had never—ever!—allowed anyone to see how badly he hurt. Yet he had, this morning, and in doing so he'd hurt her with his behavior.

Cursing her unreasonable attitude toward the books, Adam opened the door, releasing a cornucopia of scents. He couldn't let a sudden attack of conscience deter him, he thought with a sniff. Max didn't want to destroy anything, he just wanted to keep it safe! Of course, what could he expect from a woman who housed a devil cat and ate flowers as if they were popcorn? He was not dealing with a rational mind, that much was obvious.

His conviction wavered. Lord, she was so beautiful!

With a growl, he told his conscience to take a flying leap, and studied the room. It was a twin in size to the bedroom, a simple boxlike interior, but filled with bunches of dried herbs hanging upside down on a multitude of drying racks. Their pungent odors wafted to him again, tickling his nose. He sneezed. Great, he thought as an allergy-induced tear trickled down his cheek, she had goldenrod in here. His head felt like an overblown balloon! He blinked and looked for something big enough to shelve books.

A long table sat beneath the window, covered

with alcohol lamps, ceramic dishes, mortars—the same kind of implements he'd seen in Max's basement stillroom. The only other piece of furniture, a double-doored cabinet, stood against the far wall. Stifling another sneeze, he limped toward it and pulled the handle. It wouldn't budge. Adam knuckled his eyes and swore fervently when he saw the worn lock. He glanced around, searching for something to use to force it, then realized he didn't want to broadcast his intentions to Diana by leaving telltale marks all over her case. And he didn't know how to pick it.

"Sub thief I ab," he muttered in a congested voice.

Telling himself she might be back any second, he decided to give up for now. Then, with a final, violent sneeze, he hobbled out and closed the door. Crawling face-first into bed, he reluctantly gave in to his fatigue.

But though his head cleared, he couldn't erase the memory of the wildcat with the hunted violet eyes. Every square inch of his body tightened, and he wondered how he would manage a cold shower in a bathtub without a showerhead and with a fanny full of little holes.

The setting sun shadowed Diana's cabin when she finally returned. Outside, she placed her heavy basket by the front door with a thump, stomped the caked mud from her boots with less than her usual enthusiasm, and wearily unloaded the shotgun and drew off her heavy jacket. It had been a productive day of foraging, but Lord, she was exhausted. One restless night on a lumpy couch certainly made a difference in her stamina, she decided, but she had little choice. Adam would hang all over the silly thing.

When she entered, Dodger wrapped himself around her ankles in an unusual show of affection, then followed as she set everything aside and trudged toward the kitchen, racking her brains for an idea for dinner. Leftover stew again just did not appeal to her, and she didn't think it would to Adam either.

After tripping over the cat once, she patiently waited for him to leap onto the counter before she continued. He sat beside two white packages and snorted soulfully.

Frowning, Diana blinked, wondering where she'd seen them before. Steaks, she remembered, from her freezer! Adam had raided her food stores.

Before she could raise her ire, she realized something else. Her cabin, normally ice-cold upon her return, was warm as toast. There was a fire dancing in the hearth, thawing food instead of leftovers, and a sexy, thoughtful man in her bed. If she were a normal woman, her life would be complete. Instead, she tried not to think about it. She simply unwrapped the steaks, set them to marinate in her own special recipe, then went toward the bedroom to thank Adam with all the dignity and grace she could muster.

"What in the hell do you think you're doing!" she shrieked when she saw him.

He glanced down from his precarious perch on a chair. "Changing a light bulb," he said, returning to his task. "How long has it been since you've been up here? There are bugs up here from the Mesozoic Era, and this kind of socket went out with the Zoot suit." He clicked his tongue chidingly. "For a self-sufficient type, you're not very good around the house."

"Get back in bed!" When he didn't move, she tugged on his sweatpants, her heart in her mouth.

"If you're trying to prove a point, you've proven it, okay? Now, please get back in bed before you start bleeding again."

He finished tightening the bolt under the fixture, then stepped down, groaning the moment his foot hit the floor.

"I knew it." She grabbed his arm and tugged.

"Oh, the pain," he murmured, his gaze downcast.

She paled. Lord, it must be excruciating! "C'mon, just a little farther." As her knee touched the bed, Adam spun her around, unbalancing her. She fell backward; he fell atop her.

"Gotcha," he whispered, his blue eyes twinkling merrily.

His bare chest and hard thighs pressed against her, but she didn't have to think of glaciers this time. Her fury rose like a brushfire. "Get off!" Shoving hard, she managed to get enough leverage to squirm from beneath him. Quickly, she sprang to her feet, her chest heaving in indignation. "I don't believe you! This is a reflex action for you, isn't it? A doctor taps your knee with a hammer, you kick. A woman gets anywhere near you, you pounce!"

"Diana, honest, it's only you, I swear!"

"Please don't. You might turn into a pillar of salt!"

"Goddess, it's just that I want you so badly. No matter how hard I try, I can't stop thinking of you and how much I want to make love with you."

His intent expression, his return to using the endearment, almost had her believing him. Almost. "Those words are curiously blasphemous in your mouth, Yankee. You don't want a baring of souls, a—a meshing of minds and bodies, you want a quick tumble and a cab ride home!"

A crooked grin spread across his face. "I'm really getting to you, aren't I?" he murmured huskily.

Her nostrils flared. "You—you—" Unable to think of a vile enough epithet, she spun around and stomped from the room.

In the kitchen, she rummaged for the meat fork, then punched the steaks repeatedly, venting her rage. She had never met such a blatantly sexual male as Adam Daniels, but his attitude infuriated her! Every time she worried about him, every time she thought there might be something in his heart besides rocks, he turned into a rutting beast! How could she even suspect anything existed beneath that juvenile exterior but a juvenile interior? "Shallow, self-serving, loathsome, shallow—"

"You said that one already."

"It bears repeating!" She glanced up at him, leaning casually against the wall beneath a shelf full of decorative baskets, then back at dinner. That rakish smile of his seemed permanently affixed to his face, damn him! Swiftly, she retrieved her basket from the porch, and dumped its contents in a colander to rinse.

"Are those asparagus tips?" he asked. At her terse nod, he sighed in delight. "And you have salad greens and potatoes. Don't deny it, I saw it all! I'm in heaven. Real food."

Diana turned away to hide a wicked grin that sprang to her mouth despite her irritation. Adam was in for a shock, but she didn't want to ruin it just yet. She wanted to savor every moment. "Did you eat the soup?" she asked sweetly. Now that she knew vengeance would be hers, she could afford to be gracious.

"I slept through lunch. Besides, I didn't want to complicate my injuries by choking on it."

Oh, no, she thought as she heard his strained, rebuking tone. She wouldn't fall for that trick twice! "No problem, we'll have a big dinner."

"Great, I'm starved."

She set the vegetables aside and pulled out the greens. When he made no further comment, she peeked at him from the corner of her eye. A tiny frown creased her brow. He really did look pale and drawn. His exertions with her must have worn him out. "Why don't you sit down? I'm used to doing this on my own."

"And I'm used to watching," he said with a wry smile. "My best friend is a gourmet cook, and he hates people in his kitchen. But thanks, I'll stand. Sitting isn't my strong point right now."

"Are you going to stand through dinner?"

"I'm seriously thinking about it." He cleared his throat. "I have a question, and it's been bugging me all morning."

"What?"

"If I lift this bandage, I won't find lumpy, moldy dough, will I?"

She sighed. "No, Adam, it's the same antibiotic ointment you'd find in a drugstore."

Tense silence stretched. "You're a strange mix, Goddess."

"I'm practical. It works better." She continued washing.

"I wish I could say I'm sorry about what happened earlier, but I'm not."

Her hand clenched, squashing the leaf. "Adam, don't."

"No, I have to say it—and from a safe distance. I'm not giving up, you know. I want you more than I've ever wanted any other woman in my life. And I know my less than subtle tactics don't help. I simply go a little crazy around you, I guess." He shrugged. "I'm healing, and you're getting better with your arctic freezes. You won't have to put up with me much longer."

Diana swallowed hard. In his own bizarre way, Adam was extremely honest. "I'll keep that in mind. Now, please sit or recline somewhere. You really do look like hell."

"In a minute, I promise. Which plant do I eat for morning breath? I think I need it after my nap."

She nodded. "The middle one." When he didn't move, she sighed, telling herself that like any sick little boy, Adam had simply run out of energy, ignoring his body's need to rest in his need for activity. Leaning over the sink, she picked one of the flowerpots off the windowsill and approached him. His skeptical look drew a chuckle from her. "It won't poison you, I promise." She held it out to him, trying not to think how close she had to stand to him to do it. As long as he made no sudden moves, she was safe. "Smell it."

With a startled glance at her, he obediently sniffed the low-growing plant. "Smells like dirt." A ghost of a smile lifted his mouth. "You don't smell like dirt."

She ran her palm lightly over the growth, releasing its fragrant oil, and placed it beneath his nose again. "Oh, really?"

The sharp, tangy odor made him start. "Peppermint!"

Diana nodded and pulled one miniscule leaf, showing it to him on the tip of her finger. "Corsican mint. Small, but potent." She placed it on her tongue, delighting as its flavor burst in her mouth. His gaze followed her movement, and her heartbeat accelerated as if she'd drunk a gallon of Nana's brew. *The North Atlantic*, she thought as she plucked another leaf and held it out to him, taking a step backward. Beneath the minty scent, she could smell her own carnation soap on his skin. *Ten-foot icicles.* "They make crème de menthe out of it," she said hoarsely. "Just suck on it."

Instead of picking it from her fingertip, his hand slowly circled her wrist, and though she tried, she couldn't find the will to pull away. His blue eyes darkened, holding her spellbound as he opened his mouth. With only a tiny hesitation, he slipped her finger inside his mouth, placing the leaf on his tongue. Then he closed his lips around her and obediently sucked.

Diana bit back a moan. *Russian steppes.* Sensation coursed through her. *Siberian winters.* He drew on her again and again, his teeth rasping against her skin.

"Adam—" she began, but he cut off her words with a kiss that curled her toes. His mouth caressed hers hungrily, coaxing at her stubborn resistance. Had she subconsciously been hoping for this? she wondered, unable to visualize another shield against the pleasure that rippled through her. Was he the one? Before she could stop herself, her lips parted, inviting his invasion.

And the entire shelf of baskets crashed down on their heads.

Four

Diana set a handful of ice cubes carefully in the towel, fighting her tears of frustration. Wordlessly, she gave the bundle to Adam, who leaned against the wall amid the clutter of fallen baskets. The shelf hung at an angle beside him. She was a fool to believe anyone could get through the safeguards around her body. No one had before, and no one ever would. "I knew something would happen."

He held the ice pack to the top of his head. "It was an accident, Goddess. You can't possibly blame yourself."

"But I do!" She glanced up at him. With his black hair squashed flat beneath the pack, he smiled gently down at her. His laughing and stoic acceptance of every disaster that had befallen him triggered a flood of remorse in her. "I do blame myself, Adam. Every time you touch me, the world goes crazy!"

"That's what I wanted to hear," he muttered, and gathered her in her arms. "Oh, baby, it's just the most wonderful—"

"You're not listening!" Diana stomped her foot. "And I'm not a baby!"

He jerked back, wincing as her foot connected with his, and he bashed his forehead on the corner of the shelf.

"See?" she said, glaring. "It happened again!"

"Diana!" He transferred the pack to the front. "You stepped on me, and I walked into it!"

"No, dammit, I'm the cause! The chair, the—the shotgun, everything! It's all my fault!"

"Dodger—"

"Dodger couldn't get up to that shelf if he prayed, Adam!"

"Oh, Goddess . . ." He reached out to her again.

She stepped back. "I have to get you out of here before anything else happens! I—I—" She swallowed hard, and wildly searched the room for her keys. "I'll drive you back to St. Louis in my Jeep and figure out a way to get your car to you."

"And how am I supposed to sit?"

Pausing, she blinked rapidly to clear her eyes and focus her mind. "You can lie down in the back or something."

"I'd never fit in the back of a Jeep, Goddess."

"I'll make you fit!" Finding her keys, she clutched them and snatched her jacket on the way to the door. "You're leaving now, before I kill you!"

He caught her before she made it. "Diana, you can't fold me up and stuff me in! What's wrong with you?"

"Everything!" She struggled in his arms. "Get away from me!"

"No. Not until you tell me why you're so hysterical."

"I am not hysterical!" Her voice squeaked, belying her words, and Adam chuckled softly. Closing her eyes tightly, she fought for control of her emotions. She breathed deeply several times, clenching and unclenching her fists. "I'm not hysterical," she repeated in a more subdued tone. "I am a rational, practical person." His body warmed against her, and she couldn't call up any frigid images to help her. Her eyes flew open, and she stiffened. "Please let me go."

"In a minute." His gentle smile almost undid her good intentions. The gashed lump on his forehead, swelling and turning purple, reminded her of the danger he was in. "First I want you to tell me what you're babbling about." Tenderly, he pushed a strand of hair away from her cheek. "I want you to tell me how a string of unrelated accidents can possibly be your fault."

Quickly, she jerked away. "I'm jinxed, dammit!"

"What?"

His expression defied belief, and she regretted her impulsive utterance immediately. "Look, I know it sounds ridiculous, but— "

"I didn't say it sounded ridiculous, Goddess. You're talking to a man who clapped louder than anyone else over Tinker Bell. I'm just surprised. For a practical person, you sure have strange ideas." His lopsided grin widened across his mouth. "I have a confession to make too," he whispered, his blue eyes intense. "Every Christmas I still sleep on the couch, convinced I'll see the jolly man himself dive down my chimney."

She lowered her gaze. "You're making fun of me."

"No, I'm not." His finger tilted her chin up, forcing her to meet his eyes. "There is magic in the world, Goddess. Sometimes we can't see it, or taste it, or touch it, but that doesn't mean it doesn't exist. It just means we have to accept it and the wonder it gives us. But a jinx . . ." He shook his head. "That's not magic, love. It's too dark. Magic is the thing that makes imagination fly. It's bright, positive—wishes granted, dreams come true—not something that hurts us."

"I never said this was magic." Her throat tightened. Good Lord, she believed he meant it! Dammit, there was something endearing about a man who still believed in Santa Claus! But she couldn't let him enchant her with his words or his mesmerizing eyes.

She turned away and shrugged off her jacket, setting her keys down carefully. Flight was a cowardly option, and she was *not* a coward. "Adam, I know there's a logical explanation for this. Brain waves, electrical impulses, phases of the moon, or something. I don't understand the reasons behind it, but I understand results. Every time I feel—" She swallowed hard—"aroused, every time you touch me, something disastrous happens."

"Coincidence."

"No. Fact." She spun to him, anguish tightening every muscle in her body as she fought it. "Do you think you're the first man to make me feel this way? I'm thirty years old, Adam, and I discovered boys long before anyone else in my family." With an effort, she lowered her gaze and turned away. "You don't know what it's like. I get so close sometimes that I can almost touch it, then pow! Defeat, snatched right out of the jaws of victory."

"I know."

She shook her head. He couldn't possibly understand what she'd gone through. "No matter how many times I've tried, I can't get past it. Dammit, I'm sick of this!"

"Are you?"

She spared a quick look over her shoulder. "If you had the drive of a rabbit, would you willingly choose a sexless relationship?" she asked him.

His blue eyes twinkled. "You're asking the wrong person."

"Yeah, I guess so." She sighed.

"You haven't asked me if I'm willing to try," he said, stepping closer.

Diana whirled away. "I'm not willing to risk it again!"

"Again?"

Steeling herself, she wandered into the kitchen to search for her grill. If she had to prove her claim to protect him, she would, though it went against her grain to divulge so much about herself. "I was married, Adam. Did you know that?"

"No," he said curtly.

"Yep. Blood tests, vows, the whole bit. And it lasted longer than any relationship I've ever had." She thumped the grill on the counter, then dumped the asparagus onto a steamer and set the pot on the stove. "A whole day."

His silence spoke volumes, and without turning to face him, she extended the metal legs and fished out the steaks. "Kyle was the nephew of the crew chief on the first real survey I'd ever done, a grant one of my professors had obtained. We were researching a nearly extinct relative of foxglove in northern Oregon, hoping it had similar properties. Digitalis, you know." She cleared her throat and carried the grill to the fireplace, setting it above the now-red embers. "He roared into camp one night on this huge motorcycle, full of fun with a devil-may-care attitude. Lord, he was gorgeous." She poked at the steaks. "To say he swept me off my feet would be a gross understatement. But I was very conscious of my problem, and no matter how many times we started something, I always stopped before it went too far."

"That must have been difficult."

"It was." She sighed, wondering how Adam would take the rest. So far he listened quietly, seemingly hanging on her every word, but how long could that last? "Kyle came up with the bright idea that it was because we weren't married, that my old-fashioned morals were subconsciously offended by our state of noncommitment. I thought he was right, and I was crazy about him. So, we went into Portland and made the arrangements and were married."

She gulped hard, unable to tell him the rest yet, then lifted the edges of the grill with two forks, carrying them quickly back to the counter. She couldn't bring herself to look at Adam. "Kyle was . . . understandably impatient on our wedding night."

"Did he hurt you, Goddess?"

Diana swallowed back the tears that rose to her eyes at Adam's tender, understanding tone. Where was the smart-mouthed rogue? She knew how to handle that Adam, how to protect them both with her anger. This Adam was far too attractive. "No, Kyle didn't hurt me. He was wonderful. But we . . ." Her fists clenched on the counter, and she deliberately relaxed her fingers before pulling the vegetables off the stove. "We, uh, didn't exactly plan it too well, forgetting about protection. And I didn't help, because I finally thought I had my jinx licked. But I didn't. He jumped on his cycle afterward, to find a drugstore, and he had a terrible accident. He pulled through. I didn't. And the rest, as they say, is history."

"History?" He gasped and limped up behind her, grasped her shoulders and turned her to him. His eyes filled with gentle humor. "Diana, you don't honestly believe that because you made love, he had an accident, do you?"

Her lower lip trembled and she bit it hard, lowering her gaze to his chest. Her heart sank, and she realized a tiny part of her had hoped for a different reaction. "Don't laugh at me, Yankee," she whispered hoarsely. "I've lived with this long enough to know what I am and am not capable of."

"I'm not laughing at you." He raised her chin, his eyes studying her face thoroughly. "I'm not, I promise. But it is a bit much to swallow, even for me."

Well, she'd told him, and he didn't understand. For some reason, it hurt. She pulled slowly away and fixed their plates, then stared at them unseeing, wondering why they didn't look right. "For pity's sake, I forgot the potatoes." She reached over to the bin.

"Don't worry about it."

She paused, helpless tears stinging her eyes. "They'd take too long, anyway," she murmured. "How about some wild rice?"

"Forget about the starch, okay? Will you tell me why you suddenly look like a squirrel staring down the barrel of a shotgun?" His hand brushed her arm, and she started. He withdrew. "Dammit, woman, talk to me!"

"Why? You don't believe anything I've said."

"I believe that you believe it. But—"

She waved her hand and sniffed. "No, it's okay. I don't blame you." What had she expected? she wondered. That he would take her in his arms and call for another mishap with his jaunty humor? Of course he'd be more likely to defy her belief. Who wouldn't? Though he obviously had some semblance of tact, she couldn't hold out any hope that a zinger wasn't forthcoming, and she had her pride, after all. She couldn't stand it if he taunted her, so she'd simply avoid the subject from now on. As soon as she'd obtained certain promises.

She straightened her shoulders and forced back her tears. "I want you to leave tomorrow."

Her misty violet eyes stabbed through Adam with a double-edged knife of pain, and the abuses to his body paled in comparison. A lump rose to his throat as he saw her vulnerability. No one had ever touched his soul like this woman, and he had the most frightening feeling that no one ever would again. Before he could stop himself, he reached out his hand. Diana flinched away, no longer icy but wary.

Hurriedly, he dropped his gaze and eased into his chair with a wince, swallowing his reaction to her sudden defenselessness. His luck hadn't thrown him a curve, it had changed the rules on him, and his own emotions were too chaotic to allow him to think clearly. Something told him Diana's problem mirrored his own in many ways, but he wasn't quite certain how. He'd seen his dreams destroyed through no fault of his own, while she blamed something inside herself for her disillusionment. A small, heretofore ignored part of his mind whispered that he had set himself up too, as Diana did. He had dreamed too high, had believed too strongly in his own fantasies. What reality could compare to that?

Ruthlessly, he silenced that quiet voice. Diana was his concern now. Her conviction about her jinx undermined his baser instincts, and even thwarted these newer, more confusing impulses. He wanted to hold her—not to make love, but to comfort, to make a kind of love from which he'd kept himself invincible in the past. He simply didn't know how to deal with any of it right now.

And to be honest, he didn't know if he ever would be able to.

"Promise, Adam."

With an effort, he shoved his uncertainty away. The only thing to do was to accede to her demands and sort out his feelings later. "Okay," he said softly. "I'll leave. As soon as I can."

"Tomorrow."

"I can barely sit, Goddess. I can't shift!"

She opened her mouth, then closed it. "Just don't touch me," she said, plopping the plates to the table.

"I'll think about it." Before she could comment, he plastered a dazzling smile on his face. "I should have guessed when I saw you cavorting with your furry forest creatures that you were no normal woman, Snow. I just didn't expect a built-in poisoned apple."

"Furry—" Her gaze flew to the kitchen window, then back to him. "You saw me this morning?"

"How could I help it?" He clenched his fist beneath the table to keep from wiping the trace of tears away. The last thing he wanted was that wary, hunted look in her eyes again. He had to fight to regain his earlier footing, uncluttered by anything like deep emotion. "What did you do? Cast a spell on them too?"

Her mouth trembled but widened. "There's a salt lick in the clearing behind the trees, Yankee. A very logical explanation. I've been working for years to overcome their natural fear of humans."

Adam picked up his utensils and cut his steak. "You almost had me fooled with that squirrel stew, you know. But I can't believe you'd hunt the animals you befriend."

"I don't." She sat at her place. "At least, not very often, and never around the cabin. It would feel like murder. But I'm very practical. I have to eat, and I don't get much in grants. I trade with some of the local hunters."

"Trade?" Grateful that Diana had apparently relaxed, and his own inner battle having ceased, Adam lifted a slice of meat to his mouth. It was delicious, and it practically melted in his mouth. But it tasted different from any other steak he'd ever had. "What do you trade?"

"Breads, jams, wild fruits and vegetables, sometimes an herbal salve or tea—never anything potentially harmful—and even recipes like the stew. There's a hunting lodge adjoining this property, and I have elderly friends a couple of miles away who trade me food for the work I do around their house. I only accept it because they wouldn't allow my help otherwise. Ev's eyesight might be failing, but he can still put meat on their table, and that's important to him."

"It still surprises me."

"I have no objection to hunting, Adam, as long as it's not done near the salt lick and it's for food, not pure sport. Most of the animals', natural enemies have been forced out of here by civilization. It helps maintain the balance."

Out of the corner of his eye, Adam saw Dodger sneaking up to the table. He put a shielding hand beside his plate and took another bite. Was it the marinade that made it taste so wonderful?

He stopped chewing as a sudden thought occurred to him. "Do you mean that stew—" He cut himself off. Dodger took advantage of his distraction to snatch the meat from his fork. Adam barely noticed. "It really was—"

Diana nodded, her violet eyes twinkling with mischief.

"Diana," he began, swallowing hard. "Uh, this steak . . . isn't beef, is it?"

She shook her head.

"I didn't think so," he muttered.

Despite his instinctive reaction, and a twinge of guilt over Bambi, Adam devoured his venison steak. It really was delicious. After dinner, he let Diana bandage his forehead, then, seeing the emotional and physical fatigue etched on her face, he overrode her protests and washed the dishes.

Diana collapsed to the sofa long before he finished. He stood looking down at her for several long moments, a puzzled frown creasing his brow. Her tumbled red hair swept her cheek; her lips, full and perfect, were slightly parted as she breathed evenly. One hand curled beneath her head, the other lay open before her. Adam reached out to her, then ran his palms along his thighs, unwilling to take the chance of waking her. He wanted to, he wanted to touch every inch of smooth skin, to feel her warmth against him, but her sheer innocence thwarted him. His goddess of the wood, his ice princess, slept with the trust of a child. The woman had held a shotgun on him, fought for her privacy with the ferocity of a wildcat, lived a lifestyle that tested her resourcefulness every minute of the day, yet she spoke with conviction of a curse, then slumbered peacefully with a potential sex maniac in her cabin.

"Who are you, Diana Machlen?" he whispered.

She made a tiny sleep sound, an intimate little sigh, and shifted her head. Swallowing a tight lump in his throat, Adam covered her quickly and hobbled to his own room. But he couldn't call on sleep as easily as she had. For hours he lay staring at a knothole on the wall beside his bed, his thoughts turbulent. What was happening to him?

Why did the image of Diana's hunted eyes linger long after she had closed them? How could a seemingly rational, practical woman actually believe she generated all of the disasters that had befallen him?

And why, against his better judgment and every tenet of bachelorhood ever unwritten, was he still here? Why didn't he just rip the pages from the damn journal and take off? The lady didn't want him here, and whether her claim of a jinx was true or not, nothing had gone right since he'd arrived. Yet he persisted in the chase against the odds, something he'd never done before. What was wrong with him?

Tomorrow, he thought, as fatigue claimed him. He'd sort it all out tomorrow.

Unfortunately, the morning brought more questions than answers. He rose late, missing Diana's dawn excursion onto the stump, and his disappointment baffled him. Her wary greeting burned him through and through, but he ruthlessly shoved his pain away, from his body and his mind. After jotting in her journal, she changed his bandages, her touch efficient and impersonal. Though he reacted to her nearness in his usual way, the hunted look in her eyes prevented him from using the situation to his advantage. Then she left, returning much later, and finally collapsing after dinner.

The next day was a repeat performance. Adam spent the day sleeping, or watching Dodger watching him, or staring restlessly at the stillroom door. Diana came home exhausted again, fixed the meal, and nearly dropped off into her plate. Tenderly, he stretched her out on the sofa, wondering if she did this every night, or if it was simply because of him.

Adam awoke the next morning feeling as if the walls were closing in on him. It was time for action. He might not understand Diana, but he still had a journal to get his hands on. And that, at least, he could do with no disasters.

The thought did not comfort him. Her key ring, lifted from beside her jacket after she'd returned her journal, burned his palm.

"Are you going to have another waffle before I leave?" she asked.

Her voice made him jump. "No, thank you. I'm stuffed." He lowered his gaze to his plate and picked at his fifth Belgian waffle with his free hand, restlessly drawing sticky magenta circles in the yellow pastry. Despite the knowledge that he had eaten venison, and squirrel stew, and Lord only knew what else, he had to admit that Diana's cooking far outdid anything he'd ever tasted. Today, she'd told him the ingredients before breakfast, obviously remorseful for springing the steaks on him. Light and crispy, the waffles contained high-protein wheat flour, rice flour, and—this one nearly stopped him—the pollen from cattails, which gave it a bright color and a strangely appealing flavor. Topping it, instead of boring maple, she'd made a homemade syrup from mulberries and wild honey. "They were delicious, Diana. Have you ever thought of dumping the research and going into business for yourself? You'd never win the Nobel, but you'd shake up the gourmet world."

"I cook to please myself, Adam. I seriously doubt if elderberry puffs will ever hit the Cordon Bleu's top ten."

"Oh, I don't know. You've obviously never tasted caviar."

Her food also gave him tremendous insight into her personality. Diana was no ice princess, but a

woman full of courage and passion—not only of
the sexual variety. The vivid colors surrounding
her in the cabin, the touchable, tastable plants,
the food made exotic with natural spices, showed
her to be a highly sensual woman. And the rugs,
set on the diagonal all over the house, told him
she wasn't nearly as balanced as she thought. But
he didn't know what to do about it, or even if he
wanted to do anything at all.

He glanced at her from beneath his brows. Diana stood at the sink, rinsing the breakfast dishes
with quick efficiency. She'd already bound her
hair, and he missed the flowing waves of flame. A
plaid flannel workshirt and worn jeans did absolutely nothing to hide her magnificent curves. After everything that had happened over the last
few days, he didn't know what to think about her,
but he fought his instinctive erotic reaction. This
was the woman who attacked him for leafing
through a book, he told himself firmly. This was
the woman who ate flowers and gathered her dinner with the morning dew, the woman who believed that she had single-handedly caused a man's
motorcycle accident from miles away with her
passion.

She turned slightly sideways, and her profile
intrigued him. But he shifted away from the images it provoked. As she turned back, he swallowed hard and, his hands muffled by a fold of his
sweatpants, he worked the only key small enough
to belong to the cabinet loose from the ring. She
might be all this and more, but she was also the
woman who valued her privacy so much she didn't
own a phone, the woman he'd shortly betray. He
almost wished she were as cold as he'd first believed. His job would be easier.

"I'm taking the Jeep today."

The key popped off, and he started, his gaze flying to the back of her head while his mouth went dry as dust. Guilty consciences were as horrible as he'd always heard. A late owl hooted outside, and he jumped again. He had to cut this out! "Well," he said heartily, "I'm certainly not going anywhere."

She paused in her rinsing, her body rigid. "Adam, I want to thank you. You've been a perfect gentleman since the other night, and I—I appreciate it."

Somewhere in the region of his heart, he felt a stab. "Don't count on it lasting forever," he said gruffly.

"You—you're really very nice, aren't you?"

Boy, did the woman know how to twist a knife! "Come over here, and I'll show you just how nice I can be." Only habit infused his tone with the proper lecherous intent, or so he told himself.

She sighed and sagged against the counter. "Now, I feel better. For a minute, I thought someone had switched you with a lookalike." She took a last swipe at a plate. "Are you sure you'll be okay while I'm gone?"

"I'm fine." He forced his best plaintive voice. "Are you going anywhere near a supermarket?"

"Maybe. I have to go into Springfield later." She glanced over her shoulder, a smile crinkling her eyes. "Having a junk-food attack?"

He shrugged elaborately. "Cheese puffs are my life."

"But this is better for you. Are you finished?" When he nodded, she collected his plate and brushed the crumbs off his quilted place mat, carefully avoiding any contact with him. "I'll be back for lunch."

"Great. More green stuff, right?"

Her smile widened to a grin. "Do you like fish?"

"Oh, thank heavens," he said with feeling. "A food I recognize." His eyes narrowed. "Wait a minute, this is a trick, right? You're talking sea horse or river slugs or something, aren't you?"

She chuckled. "How about bluegill? With biscuits and strawberry jam. My friend Weena makes the best biscuits in the entire state."

"I'll believe it when I see it."

"And I thought I was the skeptical one." She washed his plate, set it to drain, then grabbed her jacket, studying the room in confusion. "Have you seen my keys?" she asked.

Squelching his screaming inner voice, Adam reached under her place mat, the keys hidden in his now-damp palm. "These?" he asked, dangling them from his fingertips. His heart began to do the flamenco.

"Thanks." By not even so much as a blink did she indicate any suspicion. Before she left, though, she eyed him with a frown. "I still don't think I should go that far. At least when I'm foraging, I'm within screaming distance."

"Diana, go!" he ordered, relief mixing with urgency in his voice. He pointed to the door, shifting slightly as he overbalanced with his enthusiasm. "You told me your friends need your help. I don't."

Reluctantly, she opened the door, then paused at the threshold. Her head tilted. "He's out late."

"Who?" Adam asked with a squeak.

"Exactly." She turned back, her smile wide again. "Hear him?" The owl's hoot sounded from far away, much deeper than Adam's. "He's a night hunter. Probably got caught up in his meal and forgot the hour." She grew pensive. "There's an Ozark superstition that says if you hear an owl, something awful is about to happen. I never figured out where that one came from. Either there were a lot of disasters back then, or a lot of quiet owls." She shook herself. "Oh, well. See you at lunch. And get some sleep. You look terrible."

Adam gulped. He didn't believe in omens either, he told himself. "Thanks for the beauty tip, Goddess. See you."

Diana closed the door carefully behind her, shooing Dodger in with her foot as she did. Before he could lose his nerve, Adam stood, ignoring the twinges from his backside—and his back and his head and his conscience—and limped to the stillroom. When he heard her Jeep roar away, he took a deep breath, whispered, "Only for you, Max," and turned the knob.

The herbal scents washed over him, and despite his held breath, his eyes began to burn, his head immediately filled. Cursing his allergy, he hobbled forward. When he reached the cabinet, he slid the key into the lock and turned it.

After several violent sneezes, he pocketed the key and stood staring at the case, indecisive once again. By no stretch of the imagination had he ever thought it would be this difficult. All he had to do was open the doors, find the proper book, and . . .

And what? He couldn't leave yet, not when sitting was still an exercise in torture. He groaned. Shifting the gears would be worse, since it was his left leg, his clutching leg, that was out of commission. If he took the journal now and hid it in his car, Diana would surely notice it missing, and then he'd have to contend with her violet eyes full of betrayal for the remaining days he spent with her. Or maybe she'd shoot him again for real. Why hadn't he thought that far ahead? As usual, his planning left something to be desired.

He shook himself. The future of Max's company rested on his actions, and he couldn't afford delay. Who knew when he'd get another opportunity like this? He would search, and when he found the right journal, he'd mark it somehow, and pick it up just before his escape.

He winced at his mind's choice of words but knew it to be true, and not only because of the theft. Some inner warning system told him that if he stayed around Diana much longer, he would be in even greater danger than her jinx could ever cause. She was the most courageous woman he'd ever known, and he didn't know how to handle that. With that frightening thought firmly in mind, he opened the cabinet.

His shoulders sagged, and he sniffed absently as he counted. Eight shelves, and each one was packed with slim volumes. Then, sighing, he decided to begin at the beginning, and reached for the top shelf.

In deference to his allergy, he carried the book to the kitchen. He assumed the formula had been written down sometime in her adult life, but based on her present journal's age—one month old—it could be anywhere in that jumble. But Diana was meticulous about certain things, so he could safely bet that they would be in chronological order. All he had to do was see how old this one was, then estimate where to look next. Easy.

Flipping through, he immediately knew this journal was far too old. Instead of Diana's firm, precise hand, Adam found a flamboyant, childish scrawl. Frowning, he rubbed his eyes and turned to the first page. It was dated almost exactly twenty years earlier, and the entry nearly leapt from the paper:

Everything scares me and I hate myself. I think there's a monster inside of me, waiting for the fear to let it loose so it can destroy everyone I love. But it's been there ever since I was born except that I didn't know it for a long time. I wish I could run and hide forever, except the island isn't very big and the only place to go is the grotto and I saw a snake there today and Annie fell out of the tree and broke her arm when I screamed. I felt awful but somehow I just got mad and yelled at her for spying on me. She started crying and Lizzie hit me for being so mean. But I'm not mean! It's just that nothing happens when I get mad. I can't stop shaking.

Nobody wants to play with me anymore, not even Tori and Lizzie, and they're supposed to be my best friends even if they are my cousins, but I don't blame them. I want to tell them how much it hurts me when something happens, but I can't because then they'll know for sure it's my fault, and they'd hate me even more. Mama says I had night terrors when I was a baby, but they went away. Maybe if I write things down, they won't be so scary anymore, but I'm going to put this in my bed so nobody reads it. I can't make things stop happening, but I can stop being scared if I try hard enough.

Drawing a ragged breath, Adam closed the book softly and returned it to the cabinet.

Five

Adam had never been prone to introspection—not because he feared what he would see, but because he'd always known what dwelt there. At least, he thought he knew. After he read Diana's journal entry, he found an ache that refused to go away, as it had so often in the past, one that over-whelmed the pain of his body. Needing to ease both pains and to clear his head, he left the cabin and headed nowhere in particular.

He walked along, his hands shoved deep into his pockets, staring blindly at nothing at all. The poignant cry of a ten-year-old girl had shown him that the scars he thought had callused his heart were as much an illusion as her cold indifference. Because they were not old or healed. One page of wavery writing had peeled away the surface skin and poked the soul of a lonely little boy, an adopted outsider who wouldn't inherit as a natural grand-son would.

"Oh, Diana," he whispered, "what are you afraid of?"

He wandered further afield, the beauties of nature not piercing his thoughts. He tried to keep his emotions at a minimum, to allow a little of Diana's logic to help him find the common thread in the woman and the girl. But a part of him wept with the child. He knew what it was like to be excluded because of something that wasn't his fault. After fantasizing for years about a family who loved him, he'd been shoved in the middle of a power struggle, with parents who merely tolerated him and sisters who resented his presence. But he had found that he could turn supposed victories into defeats, to deflect spiteful attacks with his acid tongue, or simply forget his unrealistic dreams and the pain they caused.

Adam frowned. He had to concentrate on Diana, and her journal provided no real solutions, just more pieces, more confusing bits that shadowed the whole. But he had one explanation for her vehement refusal to surrender the books. These journals were Diana's security blanket. By using them to distance herself, she retained her perspective. By holding on to the books, she warded off the fears she felt led to disaster, trying to dispel them in the process. But her logic was faulty. An imaginative child, Diana had reinforced her beliefs every time instead of explaining them away. Didn't she understand that?

If he'd been given a comforting outlet, what would he have done? Would he hold on to it into adulthood, as she did, against all rational arguments?

The answer was a resounding no. Unlike Diana, he had learned to forget the past and refused to plan for an uncertain future. Allowing his hopes to build to the breaking point, as she did her fears, only led to disillusionment. But he could sympathize with her motives, and he knew he would never take the journal away from her, not even for Max. Diana's vulnerability went far deeper than he'd ever imagined. Though he didn't fully understand her reasons, he recognized that her need went far beyond Max's, or even his own. Somehow, the child was inextricably bound to the woman.

But how? Did sex frighten her, or was it something more, something beyond the act? What was she afraid of?

He had to help her, for both their sakes. Because . . . because . . . he took a deep breath.

Because he was falling in love with her.

"Well, I'll be damned," he whispered. The feeling was frightening, like stepping out of his skin into a harsh world. Though he felt raw and exposed without his scars, it was also exhilarating, as if he'd suddenly shoved off a mountainside on a downhill run.

He laughed. "Boy, can I pick 'em!"

"Beg pardon?"

Startled, Adam glanced up. Standing before him was a wizened female elf, dressed in a pink polyester leisure suit and leaning on a walker. He blinked, wondering if his obsession had turned to madness, but she was still there. "Hi," he said blankly.

"Hi, yourself," she said, giving him a suspicious stare. "What are ya doin' here, stranger? Ya lost?"

He looked around him, stunned to realize that he'd walked miles from Diana's cabin. He stood at the edge of the forest, beside a neat white cottage. "I think so. Where am I?"

"The Ozarks."

Diana wasn't the only wary beast in the woods, he thought, and called up his best smile. "I mean, where exactly? I left Diana Machlen's place, and suddenly I'm here."

Her face cleared immediately. "You must be the Yankee! Why, you just missed Diana. Matt called, over to the lodge. He shut down for good, you know, but Nathan, his hired hand, is down with the influenza, and she helps out sometimes, but she'll be there all morning if I know Matt." She shook her head, her raisin-brown eyes twinkling. "Oh, the stories I hear about you!"

He swallowed a chuckle. "My fame has spread. And you are?"

"Jest call me Weena, honey. Any friend of Diana's is a friend of mine."

"She told you I was a friend?"

"Well," Weena whispered, "she said you got shot over to her place and were staying with her for a while. High time too, I say! She needs a man around. All that stompin' through the bushes, carin' for ever'body in sight, and nobody to take care of her." She *tsked* at this unreasonable attitude.

"What else did she tell you?" he asked, sensing an excellent source of information.

"Not much. Diana, she don't give much away."

His shoulders sagged. "No, she doesn't, does she?"

"She's powerful generous, mind you, and I love her like a daughter. Don't laugh enough, though. Takes everything too serious." She frowned. " 'Cept my stories."

"His ears perked up. "What stories?"

"Haints. Ghosts. See, these hills are older'n time itself, and around here we take pride in our tales. But Diana only wants to hear about the herbs and such. Shoot, you can't have one 'tout the other!"

He filed that away. "I would love to hear your stories, Weena."

" 'Bout time I had an appreciative audience. Won't Diana jest holler when she finds out about this!"

Adam hesitated. If she found out he'd been asking questions about her, Diana would blow a gasket. Besides, he wanted to get to know this woman without any of Diana's interference. Weena was beautiful, earthy, and uncomplicated, like the very hills around them. "Why don't we keep this our secret, Weena? If Diana knew I was wandering around with my injuries, she might just give me another of those nasty potions of hers."

"True enough. That girl has the healer's gift, and she don't like her patients to decide for themselves. Real bossy."

"That's Diana." The thought of her going head-to-head with Emma made him shudder. They'd feel the reverberations all the way to Alaska, if those two ever got together. It was going to take a fine bit of luck to protect Diana, Emma, Max, *and* the journals—and a lot of verbal dancing to convince Emma he could—but he had to try. The last thing any of them needed was for his friends to storm the place right now. "Do you have a phone?"

"Sure! You're welcome to use it anytime." Weena turned her walker. "Enough gabbin' out here, Yankee. Come on in and set yourself down." She stopped and grinned at him. "Oh, I guess that'll be kinda difficult, won't it?"

He bowed, his mouth lifting, then followed, keeping pace with her slow movement. "Now don't you worry your pretty little head about me, Weena. I'm a big boy."

She crowed. "Oh, with that smile, I bet you like 'em racy! And I got a doozy for you! Unrequited passion and ever'thing. Diana, she listens but don't understand, you know?"

"But won't Ev be scandalized that his wife is telling a stranger"—his voice lowered—"racy tales?"

She scoffed. "Ev is out in his bog. He wouldn't notice if I stripped nekkid and went to a costume ball as Lady Godiva."

"His loss, my gain. Perhaps you'll save a dance for me, madam."

"Dance? Me?"

"Of course! Haven't you ever heard of chair dancing? You sit, I stand. It's the latest rage, I promise!"

She cackled madly. "You and me's gonna get along jest fine."

Adam learned nothing more from Weena, but he departed with his spirits considerably lifted. Emma had promised to back off, at least for a while, and Weena was a delight. He'd never seen a more spritelike woman. She might be nearly crippled, but her attitude was marvelous, and she cooked like a dream. Her hands had responded first to the medication the doctors had given her. He had a suspicion Diana's care did even more. Weena had confided that though she and Ev had moved back to her birthplace on retirement, she missed the hustle of teaching and raising a family, and Diana's visits relieved the boredom she suffered from.

And Weena had helped him. She had shown Adam that happiness did more than the best doctors in the world. All the way home, though his body screamed from the walking he'd done, his light heart almost made him forget his injuries. And Weena's stories had given him the germ of an idea.

When he reached the cabin, he sniffed the soup he was supposed to eat and put it on to heat. After a small disagreement with Dodger, Adam went to his car, hoping he'd packed a copy of a magazine with the perfume ad in it. For the first time in his wayward life, he had found a dream worth fighting for, and he had the feeling Diana's portrait might show him more than he'd originally thought. After all, he thought with a grin, legends had a core of scientific truth.

Diana sloshed through the murky water, her borrowed hip boots snug against her calves, and reached for the last young cattail. The wind blew it away from her hand with an almost human sigh, reminding her of one of Weena's more mischievous "haints."

"Nonsense," she whispered, and tightened her grip on her knife. One of Matt's horses whinnied, seeming to laugh at her attempts, and her eyes narrowed. She steadied herself on the muddy lake bottom, lunged for it, and caught the swaying stem. With a sense of triumph, she lopped off the yellow-green top and stored it in the heavy bag at her side, then decided she had enough for dinner and exited the lake.

After she returned the boots to the lodge, she retrieved her fish and biscuits from the industrial kitchen, twitched some of the black dustcovers back in place over the furniture, then pulled the heavy main door closed behind her. For a moment, she lingered, caressing the carvings with a smile. Some artisan had had a field day with this one—every mythical creature known to man roared or rampaged across the wood in wild abandon. There was a time in her life when it would have given her nightmares. Now, she could appreciate the beauty and care that had gone into such meticulous work. She hoped whoever bought it from Matt cared for it as he had.

Shaking herself, she strode to her Jeep, loaded everything into it, and roared off. As she slowed for the first turnoff, she rolled her head and shoulders, easing her aching muscles. She had mucked out the stables, picking up the slack Nathan's absence had caused. Though she'd never mastered the art of riding even the gentlest of the horses he kept for some of the more adventurous hunters, she knew what went where and could saddle one almost as fast as Nathan now. She wondered if the next owner would keep them, then shoved the thought from her mind.

The delicious aroma of biscuits mingled with the faint odor of fresh fish, filling her Jeep. She smiled crookedly. Weena had given her enough bluegill to feed an army—even Matt had laughed when she'd stowed it all in his industrial-sized refrigerator while she was there. Generous to a fault, that lady. Adam would probably adore her too. If he—

No, she reminded herself firmly, she didn't want Adam there, or anywhere else. He'd be gone soon enough. She didn't need the temptation he presented, and she definitely didn't need the aggravation or the guilt she felt over his injuries. Despite his cocky attitude, Adam would turn tail just like everyone else she'd ever known. After a few more "accidents," he would believe her, and would run like hell. Who in his right mind wouldn't? What kind of masochist would hang around and not just await, but actually ask for, the pain she caused? Only an idiot, that's who. And only an idiot would wish that he would.

Diana pulled into her driveway and parked. To her surprise, she found Adam rummaging in his car, flinging items over his shoulder, uncaring, into the dirt. Sighing inwardly, she dodged a tennis ball, stepped over several assorted oddities—a stuffed chicken with a bouncy spring neck, a squashed baseball cap, and the ragged head of a doll—and tapped him. He jerked and smacked his head on the sunroof, yowling when it hit the same place the shelf had. Diana snatched her hand back. "Sorry."

" 'S okay." He backed out carefully.

"What in the—" She cut herself off as his outfit penetrated. Other than a pair of moth-eaten shorts and his unzipped brown leather bomber jacket, he wore nothing but an apron and a gentle smile. His wide chest was lightly filmed with perspiration, a small scar she hadn't noticed before stood stark against his flushed skin. The scattering of ebony hair swirling around and between the dark male nipples made her pulse race. Why, when she'd seen him naked, did glimpses of his half-covered body do as much—if not more—to incite her raging hormones? "What happened to your sweatpants?"

"I spilled milk all over them. But I won't cry over what's past." With a lopsided smile, he climbed between the seats.

Something in his tone indicated a double meaning, which baffled her. She waited for an explanation, but he offered none. "What are you doing?" she asked finally.

"Looking for something."

She huffed. "That's obvious. What are you looking for?"

He pulled out and slipped another cap over her French braid, tugging the bill down over her brow.

"Just something." With a grin, he kissed the tip of her nose and opened the back hatch.

She tilted her head back and eyed him with a frown. "You're moving a lot easier," she commented, more to fill the silence than anything.

He froze. "I'm very good at hiding my pain?"

She smiled wryly and lifted the cap, smoothing the emblem. "Don't worry, I'm not going to kick you out. You'll leave on your own soon enough."

He glanced around to her. "Why are you so convinced I'll—"

She cut him off by showing him the cap and raising her brows.

"I see." One corner of his mouth lifted. "Don't depend on past performance, Goddess. I may surprise you yet." He returned to the trunk.

"I don't like surprises."

"But I do. Are you going out again?"

"Why?"

"Just wondering."

Inexplicably disappointed by his seeming wish to get rid of her, she set the cap on the passenger seat. "Actually, I am. I gathered some more pieces of the tonic this morning, so I could have fresh as well as dried, and I forgot them. I have to drive up to Springfield to drop them off at the university for analysis, and I may as well get groceries. But no cheese puffs!"

"I'll survive."

She picked up the other objects and returned them to the car, puzzled. "I pictured you with Italian suits and thousand-dollar watches, not a Mickey Mouse clock."

"That was a present from Max—my fifteenth birthday. He said since I lived in a Mickey Mouse household, I should learn to tell the correct time. I

agreed one hundred percent, and left on my six-
teenth birthday."

Something inside her clenched. "I wasn't trying
to pry, Adam. Sorry."

"You weren't prying. Lovers tell each other things
like that."

Her breath caught. "What did you—we're not
lovers!"

"Not yet, but we will be. I could tell you more, if
you want."

"No! I don't—"

"—want to know. Yes, you say that a lot."

She wanted to ask him about the strange objects, to peek over his shoulder into the car, but
she couldn't bring herself to do it.

"Ah-ha!" He shot a wary look around the raised
lid and stuffed something inside his jacket, something that crackled. "Are you hungry?"

"What are you hiding?"

"None of your business." He pursed his lips
playfully. "For someone who doesn't like information, you sure are nosy."

She gaped as he limped past her into the cabin.
Hurriedly, she grabbed her parcels from the Jeep
and followed. When she entered, he stood at the
stove. His jacket lay slung over the back of a chair.
She picked it up. Nothing fluttered to the floor.
She glanced around, but nothing seemed out of
place, and she set her coat over his. "Adam, what
are you up to?"

He flourished a large spoon. "Heating up soup
for lunch. Once I figured out it's chicken, I felt
this horrible stab of hunger." He paused. "It *is*
chicken, isn't it?"

"Yes, but—I don't mean at the stove, what did
you have?"

He held his hand to his forehead. "Oh, the pain."

Her eyes narrowed. "I told you not to play on your injuries forever, Yankee."

"Not forever. Just until I get what we want."

"You're talking in riddles," she said with a growl. "And you're pushing your luck."

"Not as much as you think," he muttered. "Besides, I've pushed it to the limits most of my life." His grip tightened on the spoon. "This time I won't let it fail."

Before she could question him, Dodger climbed up her pant leg to her shoulder, then down her arm, reminding her she still held the fish. She tried to shake him off, but his claws found a firm grip on her sleeve. Wincing, she deposited the package in the refrigerator, and Dodger bit her wrist for her betrayal.

She lifted her arm and glared at him. He touched his nose to hers, showing her he didn't hold a grudge, then sprang away. She smiled tolerantly.

"You don't snap at *him* every time he bites you."

Startled, she glanced at Adam. "Why would I? He's had a rough life. He's only reacting from instinct."

"Yet when I do, you threaten me."

She frowned. "I don't want to hurt you."

"Then let's try a little experiment. A scientific experiment." He limped up to her. "My instinctive reaction to your presence is this." Swiftly, he tilted her chin up and kissed her firmly.

She jerked back, her eyes narrowed.

"See? Cause and effect. No disaster, no—"

He cut himself off as something hissed behind them. They both turned to the stove, where the chicken soup was happily bubbling over.

"So much for science," he muttered, wrinkling his nose at the odor. He snatched the pot and threw it in the sink, then spun back to her. "We need to counteract magic with magic, Goddess."

"You're making absolutely no sense at all!" Diana stomped to the stillroom, confused and hurt by his actions, and began stuffing the tonic's separate elements into plastic bags.

"I think I'm making perfect sense!" he called.

When she completed her task, she picked up the ingredients and carried them to the table, ignoring Adam completely. She emptied the young cattails into the colander and put the bags into her sack.

Before she could turn, Adam slipped her jacket over her shoulders. "And your keys," he said, dropping them into her pocket with a jingle. "You're so defensive sometimes," he murmured.

His hand lingered on her back, and she spun to him, gripping her rucksack, prepared to swing it at him.

The angry words caught in her throat. A small, puzzled frown creased her brow as she stared at him, wondering at his new approach. Or was it only tactics? He was the same jaunty rogue, this Adam, yet he wasn't, and she couldn't pin down the difference. His blue eyes bore through her, mesmerizing her again, snatching the breath from her lungs. There was a new element, she realized, in his eyes, in his tone. He reached out and caressed her with a tenderness that made her ache. Beneath the twinkle was something new, something that said, "It's all right, I understand." And she had the oddest feeling that he did.

His warm body nearly touched hers. Her skin felt electrified, the hair on her arms standing as rigid as her nipples. Adam wasn't a sorcerer, he was a magnet—all of her armor yearned to spring from her soul, but after the years of wearing, it didn't know how anymore.

He tugged gently, but she couldn't let go, of her rucksack or her emotions. Tears blurred her vision.

"Are you that superstitious, Goddess?" he murmured. "Do you believe omens so much?"

Swallowing hard, Diana almost nodded. From the very first day, she'd wondered what it would be like to make love with this man, to lose herself in a tangle of bodies and meshing of souls that she'd never experienced. She wanted to—Lord, how she wanted to!

"Don't give that owl the satisfaction of a really catastrophic event," he whispered. "Calm down."

"Owl?"

"Of course." His eyes widened, and the corner of his mouth lifted. "Unless there's another omen I should know about?"

He made it a question, one she didn't want to answer. As if waking from a trance, she jerked. The owl, not the coffee ring! "For pity's sake," she muttered, lowering her gaze. "If you want to get technical, the bad luck's happened anyway."

Without another word, she stormed past him and out the door. His limping step sounded hollowly on the porch behind her. Adam caught her arm halfway across the clearing. "Let me go, Yankee." When he didn't, she raised tortured eyes. "Dammit, Adam, I thought we settled this!"

He shook his head slowly. The faint breeze lifted tendrils of his black hair, sending it dancing on his cheeks. "We settled nothing, Goddess, except that you think you can keep me away with an invisible shield." His crooked smile warmed his blue eyes. "Everyone knows that if you disbelieve an illusion, it vanishes."

Diana swallowed hard and dropped her gaze. "I

wish it were that easy." She relaxed the fist she had unconsciously made. Her keys left painful imprints in her palm. "I have to go."

"You can't run forever, Diana."

"I'm not running. I told you, I'm jinxed. I have no choice."

"Everyone has choices."

She sighed. "Why am I arguing with you? You don't even believe me."

"I believe that *you* believe it, Goddess, but it makes no difference." He eased the pressure on her arm, but not enough to let her bolt. "I don't give up easily."

Diana looked to the shadows of the mountains beyond the ridge. Something stung her eyes. "Didn't you give up on your job? And baseball?"

His hand dropped. "You don't know anything about that."

"You're right. And I don't want to know." Clearing her throat, she strode toward her Jeep. His off-rhythm footsteps crunched behind her. "Go home, Adam."

"And why don't you want to know, I wonder?" he asked, ignoring her command. "Why haven't you asked me any questions? Do you realize I've been here for days, and you don't even know how old I am, where I grew up?" His steps halted. "If I'm married?"

Diana stopped, a tight knot forming in her chest. She'd never considered . . . "Are you—"

"No." He walked around in front of her, tilting her chin up to force her to meet his gaze squarely. "I'm thirty-two years old, I grew up mostly in Kansas City, I don't have any children that I know of, or any other blood relatives, actually. I've never been married . . ." His mouth softened, his blue eyes became intense. "And I've never wanted a woman as much as I want you."

Her pulse raced at his touch. She pulled away with an effort. "Now, I understand," she said with a forced smile. "Disbelieve an illusion, right? Never, huh? When pigs fly!" She clamped her trembling lips together and spun away.

"Why is that so hard to believe?" he asked, following again. "Oh, I'll admit I sowed a few wild oats—"

"You probably seeded the entire state!"

"—but that kind of life-style loses its allure pretty quickly."

"Right."

He barked a short, triumphant laugh. "Now, I get it! Oh, Diana, you are so transparent."

Her fists balled, and she picked up her pace. The edge of the clearing had never seemed so far away. "If you say, 'Golly, gosh, you're jealous,' I'll shoot you."

"I wouldn't be so trite. You're not jealous, Diana. You're afraid."

Both of them halted. Her blood rushed in her ears. Livid, she whirled on him. He stood, arms folded across his chest, a smug smile creasing his face. "Of all the egotistical, pompous . . ." She threw her sack at him, but it fell short of the mark. It bounced past his foot, scattering tiny bags in the dirt.

"Temper, darlin'. After all that healthy food, we can't have you rupturing an artery, can we?" His smile widened. "You're scared to death that you'll fall in love with me, aren't you?"

"Me? Afraid of you, Yankee? Don't make me laugh." Her attempt sadly lacked force.

He stepped nearer, tilting his head, undaunted by her hostility. "Where would your magic shield be if you did love me, I wonder? How could you protect yourself without it?"

"There's no such thing as magic!" She backed away from him. "And I'm not protecting myself, I'm protecting you, you idiot!"

Tense silence fell between them. Something flickered across his face, just for an instant. "I think you like believing that, but I don't think it's entirely true. Have you ever heard of a griffin? It's a beautiful, fierce creature, not ugly or evil, and deep down inside you have one locked inside bars of the toughest iron you can find. But you know what else?" His blue eyes bored into her. "I think you're dying to unlock that cage."

"You don't know what you're talking about," she told him, her throat rasping around the words.

"I think I do." His voice dropped to a whisper, and he took her shoulders in a firm grip. "It's there, waiting to spread its wings and soar to the skies, and that scares the hell out of you." He caressed her chin in a quick, tender stroke. "Don't be afraid of it, Goddess, it won't hurt you. It just wants its freedom."

She opened her mouth, then closed it tight.

"Let it loose, love."

She wanted to shove him away again. She wanted to stop her ears from hearing his words, to tell him it was an illusion too.

And yet . . . before she could halt it, something began to grow inside, an awakening of a kind she'd never experienced. Like the first rosy streaks of dawn on the horizon with a promise of a beautiful day to come, it spread through her, tentatively, waiting for an obstruction. It was a little frightening, but exhilarating too, and she couldn't halt its birth any more than she could prevent the new day. Never had she ever felt this before, and it went way beyond the bounds of chemistry.

Diana drew a deep breath. "I have to go," she said, numbly stuffing the packets back into the sack. "These are important. They have to be analyzed. And I—I have to do the grocery shopping. I'm out of—something." She shook her head, wrestling inwardly with this new threat. "The list is in the Jeep."

"I'll be waiting," he murmured huskily.

She just nodded. Resisting the urge to bolt, she left with her normal stride, outwardly calm, casually serene.

But the new sunrise part of her trembled.

Six

After dropping her herbs at the university lab, Diana caught herself crossing her fingers, swore, and headed for the supermarket. Normally, she could zip through in ten minutes flat. The staples she bought quarterly—flour, salt, sugar, dish soap, toilet paper, a few extra spices—those were easy to find, and the choice was hardly dawdling material. Today, however, the place was a jungle, with danger lurking around every corner.

She hovered at the bakery, drooling over éclairs. She drifted into the cookie aisle twice, with no memory of how she got there. She placed two bags of cheese puffs in her basket before she caught herself, and later she literally yanked a gallon of ice cream out of one hand with the other.

By the time she reached the checkout, her fingers trembled, her palms sweat, and her hair hung in disarray after she'd repeatedly twiddled with it to keep from grabbing every empty calorie she could find. Tired and irritable, she felt as if she had just spent a month in the harshest survival camp in the world, and she hadn't passed the final exam.

"For pity's sake," she growled as she stomped out with her groceries. "You couldn't even stick to the basics, could you?" Giving it a glare of pure loathing, she loaded the chocolate fudge cake into her Jeep and roared off with a screech of tires.

Instead of heading home, she drove into the heart of the Springfield shopping district and parked. With no real purpose in mind, she wandered the streets, peeking into windows decorated with fake grass and stuffed Easter bunnies, until many sported "Closed" signs, as the sun began to set.

Finally, she tore herself away from a lingerie store with a curse and strode purposefully toward her car. Damn Adam and his talk of caged beasts! She would not dither all day because of some flip evaluation! He was wrong! She was *not* afraid of him! She wasn't afraid of anything anymore, especially some Yankee scoundrel with a libido in overdrive. From day one, he'd been all over her like a rash. This was simply another salvo in his efforts to get her into bed, that was all. And it wouldn't work, not if she had anything to say about it!

Eyes narrowed, she raced home, venting her spleen with a quick dash down a shortcut, straight through the woods and over the ridge. Wrestling with a bucking four-wheel drive had a definite advantage over manslaughter, she decided, and when she pulled into her driveway, she could even smile at his tactics. He liked surprises? Well, she'd give him one, all right. She would walk into the cabin and calmly fix dinner, completely unaffected by his psyche-out technique. And she would feed that cake to the raccoons before he even knew she'd bought it! Shoulders squared and chin firm, she carried the bags to the cabin. We'll see who cracks first, she thought, and pushed open the door.

Just over the threshold, she paused in momentary confusion. No lamps lighted the dim shadows of the room, only the flicker of firelight. The aroma of fresh biscuits filled the air, and Dodger didn't spring out in greeting. But Adam's Porsche sat in its usual spot, so he couldn't have gone. Where was he?

"Hello, Goddess."

His husky voice sent a signal flare of warning to her brain. The only time he ever used that tone was just before he jumped her or imparted some seductive tidbit about the state of his body. Warily, she peeked around the edge of the door.

Her heart lurched, and she nearly dropped the groceries. Two glasses of ruby wine sat on the hearth in front of the mesh screen, surrounded by chunks of bread and cheese. Every pillow she owned was scattered on the floor before the fireplace; sheets hung suspended from the ceiling. In the middle of it all lounged Adam, still in his shorts, and yet it wasn't the same man she'd left earlier. Diana swallowed hard. His eyes smoldering blue flames, his raven hair hidden beneath a burnoose of flowing white linen, he was her deepest fantasy.

"Welcome home," murmured the sheikh.

Adam wanted to crow in triumph when he saw the stunned expression on her face, but he resisted the urge. It wouldn't be in character. Instead, he stood slowly, never relinquishing her gaze, and paced toward her. " 'A loaf of bread, a jug of wine, and thou,' " he said, and nearly kicked himself for the trite quotation. Dammit, for once in his life he didn't want to blow a plan!

She didn't appear to mind the cliché. Her head tilted as he neared, her eyes unable to follow his without looking up, but her chin remained in the same place. Lifting a one-cornered smile, he placed his finger beneath her jaw and closed her mouth. It drifted open again. Never one to question his luck, he shrugged and leaned down to press his lips to hers, to explore the tender inner flesh with his tongue. Instead of tearing away, as he'd expected, Diana gave a tiny moan and pressed closer, crackling the paper she held in her arms.

His reaction was instantaneous. Every nerve ending flared to life beneath the costume, every molecule in his body cried out with wanting her. He buried his fingers in her hair and pulled her to him, crushing her mouth with his in a kiss that sent the blood pounding in his ears. Time ground to a halt as a violent need as old as the mountains overtook them both.

They broke at the same moment and stared at each other, chests heaving in the wake of passion. Diana's eyes flashed in fury. His own eyes widened in wonder. "Holy mother," he whispered in awe. "When that beast rages, it really rages, doesn't it, Goddess?"

She threw a bag of groceries at him. He sidestepped easily and caught the other before she could fling it. "What's this?" he asked, smelling chocolate. He peeked inside despite her mutinous expression, and grinned. "A cake?" He *tsked*, chiding her gently. "Why, Diana, whatever came over you?"

"It's for Crockett," she told him airily.

His grin widened. "You're blushing!"

"In a pig's—"

He dropped the bag and kissed her once more. Though this one lacked the desperation of the first, it was just as devastating, to him anyway. Diana took a swing at him. He caught her wrist, feeling his amusement trickle away. His voice lowered ominously in a warning that was pulled from his soul. "I won't let you fight me again, Goddess. Now that I know what you're capable of, you'll never convince me that you don't want me as much as I want you."

Her mouth worked, but she met his gaze defiantly. "I don't want you hurt, you stubborn Yankee!"

"And I don't need a self-sacrificing martyr. No one decides my fate anymore but me." His words stung her, he could see it in her eyes, and he gentled his hold on her, softening his voice. "If it's truly my welfare you're worried about, Goddess, I have just lifted that burden from your shoulders. I'm willing to take the risk. The question is . . ." He slid his hand to hers and kissed it lightly. ". . . are you?"

Diana dropped her gaze, fighting to continue breathing in a place that didn't seem to have any oxygen. Despite her inner qualms, the feeling that had begun to blossom inside of her continued to grow, and she finally realized what it was—hope. For once in her life, she had found someone who knew about her jinx and barely flinched when disaster overtook him, whose searing desire made hers look like a Boy Scout cookout in comparison. Did she really want to kill the only chance she might ever have to experience something that a cruel mix of genes had denied her? Whether it was brain waves or an honest-to-God curse didn't matter anymore. What mattered was that she had a taste of possibility, and it was sweeter than chocolate cake.

She didn't understand his motives, not completely, but she understood the results. Instead of being repelled by her, Adam kept battering at her defenses, hitting her most vulnerable points every time. For a moment, she had resented him for his accuracy; now, she didn't know what emotions whirled through her. But she needed this chance as much as she needed food and water, and she would be lying to deny it.

Her fists clenched. "I don't know what's wrong with me. All my life, I've fought for what I want, Adam. All my life, I've done my best to create something I can be proud of, to—to carve my own brand of peace and balance in a family that would overwhelm anybody. All my life I've—" Her voice broke.

"It's okay, Goddess," he said gently. "Tell me."

She pried her fingers open and cleared her throat. "The point is, I thought I'd finally found it here. I thought I had found the kind of serenity that Nana had." She hung her head. "But maybe I've been kidding myself."

"Diana . . ." He framed her face with his palms and tilted her head up. "You are your own worst critic, you know that? You don't give yourself any credit at all. You are a born fighter, Goddess, and I admire that more than you will ever know."

She closed her eyes tightly, and turned away. She didn't want his admiration. She didn't deserve it. Taking her courage firmly in both hands, she decided it was time to be honest, with him at least. "I'm just not sure I can fight you anymore," she whispered.

"What?"

She met his astonished gaze. "You confuse me. You make me feel—" She fought the tears that suddenly burned her eyes. "I don't know exactly what you make me feel, except that my body's on fire every time you're around."

"That's a start," he said. "But is it enough?"

"I don't know." She plastered on a wavering smile and faced him. "But I've never met anyone as hardheaded as you. If you're willing to take the risk, who am I to stop you?"

"You still could," he told her. "But don't do it for my sake, any of it. If you really don't want this, because *you* don't want this, then you tell me."

Her lip trembled, but she forced it steady. "Backing off so soon, Yankee? What's the matter, didn't you think I'd call your bluff?"

"I never bluff, Diana. Never."

"Then what are you waiting for?" She drew a ragged breath. "Seduce me."

A slow smile crept across his face. "I love an easy woman." He kissed her lightly then tugged her toward the pillows.

If Diana had expected any awkwardness in him, she was to be disappointed. Adam showed no hesitation as he sprawled before the fire, other than a quick wince as he hit the floor, while she dropped like a rock into the cushions. The hand that held out a wineglass to her didn't tremble, like hers, and he sipped the liquid slowly, instead of gulping it hastily as she did.

"Will you relax?" he muttered with a grin. "I'm not going to eat you." His eyes twinkled. "On second thought, that's always a possibility."

She drained her glass with a gulp and held it out. "More."

Adam's mouth twitched as he obviously fought outright laughter, but she didn't care. He refilled her glass, then halted it as she jerked it toward her. She raised inquiring brows.

"I don't want you drunk, Goddess," he told her solemnly. "I won't rush you, I promise, but I want your senses fully awake and alive. You, more than anyone I've ever known, need to savor every moment."

"Do you honestly think I would pass out on a couple of snorts of elderberry wine?" she asked.

"Is that what this is?" He stared at it, the firelight casting dancing flames deep inside it, then back at her. "It's not as sweet as I thought it would be, but yes, I think a couple of snorts of this, with you as tired as you obviously are, would put you under the proverbial table."

She smiled, but lowered her glass. "I've survived Ev's mountain maiden's breath, so this is nothing."

He choked. "His what?"

"Moonshine," she explained. "It'll burn the hairs out of your nostrils."

"People still make that stuff? Isn't it illegal?"

"Not if you don't make enough to sell. Ev makes a couple of extra jugs for his friends, but mostly he makes it for his bursitis."

"The hills are alive . . ." he murmured.

Her smile tightened. "He's also on a grant from a petroleum company. Ev's a retired chemical engineer, working on an experimental methane fuel."

Adam rolled on his stomach, propping his chin on his fist. "You are the most defensive creature," he commented with a lazy grin. "I wasn't attacking your friends, Goddess. I want to know everything about them, and how you fit into their lives. Please, tell me."

Her momentary indignation receded in the wake of his interest. "Well, Ev—"

"Wait, not like that."

Before she could do more than exclaim wordlessly, Adam pulled her to her back, her head directly beneath his. Her feet hung off the cushions, on the side opposite his. He kissed her softly, upside down, then leaned toward the hearth.

"What are you doing?" she asked in confusion.

"Open your mouth."

She did automatically, and he fed her a bit of cheese.

"Now, tell me."

Tangy cheddar, warm from the fire, melted against her tongue as she chewed. It was one of the few vices she indulged, since cheese had calcium, but she eyed him suspiciously. "I thought this was supposed to work the other way around."

"What? You want to seduce me?" He waggled his brows. "I could live with that, but I'm not Adam anymore." His chin lifted. "I'm Sheikh Ali Ben-Gay, ruler of all I survey."

"Then shouldn't I feed you, O scourge of the living room?"

"We're very liberated in Aba Daba, my little pomegranate. I'll feed, you talk."

Diana giggled, and though she wanted to blame the wine, she knew it was an intoxication that only Adam could make her feel. "Do you know how difficult I find it to speak rationally to a man wearing a pillowcase on his head?"

His expression became wounded. "I'm offended, my dove. It's the latest fashion." He waved his bandaged hand at the sheets hanging from the ceiling. "And these silks, speedily delivered from the bottoms of the choicest worms, woven by the purest hands in the Orient—"

"Percale, Yankee, and flowered at that. From the—" She frowned. "Where does that come from?"

He popped a crust of bread into her mouth without breaking stride. "Tiny percales, springing from rock to rock in the highest Andes mountains."

"That's llamas, and they make angora sweaters."

"Goats."

"What?" She chewed meditatively. One side was nearly toasted from the heat of the fire. "Oh, you're right. Llamas are mohair, right? Or is that alpacas?"

He brushed the hair from her brow and smiled down at her. "How would I know? I'm a sheikh, not a merchant. I buy others' wares, my sweet camel."

She grimaced. "Oh, puh-lease."

"Sorry, I'm running out of desert endearments."

"I kind of like Goddess," she told him, and nearly smacked herself for the admission.

"So do I," he murmured.

When he leaned over, her lips met his naturally, with only a trace of her earlier nerves. "You taste like wine," she commented.

His eyes twinkling wickedly, he dipped his fingers in his glass and dribbled the ruby liquid onto her waiting tongue. Their gazes locked, and the blue eyes darkened. Moving slowly, he licked a stray drop from the corner of her mouth. "So do you," he murmured. "You're delicious, Goddess."

His shift in mood was almost too fast for her. "I thought you didn't want me drunk," she whispered, her voice a mere thread of sound.

"If you pass out, you won't have far to fall." His lips nuzzled her ear, his breath warm.

Shivers scattered all over her body; her heart began to thump madly. "Is that why we're on the floor?"

He shook his head, his flowing burnoose falling around her face to enclose them in a private cocoon. "They don't have beds in tents." His tongue followed her jawline. "Only miles of deep, soft cushions that nearly swallow the bodies pressed into them, as they swallow each other. Locked in passion, suckling sweet beads of desire from breast, from thighs, they cry out in ecstasy with completion."

A moan built in her throat as his hand easily freed the first button of her shirt, his touch leaving a trail of fire on her skin. "Silks, wine, bread. You do things right in Aba Daba, don't you?"

"The magic is the night," he whispered against her mouth. "Only the best for my one true love."

"I'm not—" His lips stopped her words, and the sensations that rippled through her at his kiss banished even the memory of the thought. All she could feel was him. All she could sense was his mouth on hers, the warmth of his breath, and she tasted the sweetness of his tongue as it delved into her.

With a sigh, she reached up, clasping his neck with one hand. He flipped the burnoose back over his shoulder, moving between her and the fire as he kissed her temple, her earlobe, her neck. With no pause, he loosed another of her buttons and brushed the swell of her breast with his fingertips, then further, beneath the edge of her bra. The contact pulled at her heart, at deep feminine places that had never known such life, such vitality, as Adam brought her.

His scent filled her, sharper and clearer than anything she'd ever experienced, as if his touch had rarefied the very air around them. Her nostrils stung from the subtle musk and smoke from the fire. . . .

Diana's eyes flew open, and she jerked back. That smoke was too strong to be from burning wood!

"Goddess, what—"

Struggling from beneath him, she rolled swiftly onto her stomach and cried out. His "burnoose" smoldered dully, and flames licked the edges. She snatched up a pillow and began beating them.

"Hey!"

"Adam, shut up! You're on fire!"

"I'm—" He glanced down and started stripping the sheet from his head with more speed and aplomb than she'd possessed. With a curse, he flung it over the screen into the fireplace. They both stared as it burst alight, then shriveled into lumpy ash. "I think percale has polyester in it," he commented with a bland nod. "Low melting point."

"It was cotton." Her voice caught. "Part of Nana's dowry." Her fingernails dug into the pillow for a moment, adrenaline, frustration, even fear, all whirling through her. Reacting instinctively, she belted him with it. "How can you be so calm, you sod! You almost burned to death!"

"I wouldn't have lost more than a bit of hair, Goddess. Try a little gratitude. It's healthier than ranting over what might have been."

She opened her mouth to say something—any-thing—but found she couldn't. Adam had a brand of courage she envied, and at that moment she hated him for it, almost as much as she hated herself for her inability to emulate it. All her life, she had battled her fears, her weakness, yet he seemed to have none at all. What was his secret?

She flung down the pillow, tears burning her eyes. "Dammit, why don't you yell!"

He frowned at her behavior. "Why?" His confu-sion vanished. "Oh, not the jinx again. Diana, I just got too close to the screen, and that thing was ancient. Dry as a bone." With a gentle chuckle, he gathered her stiff body in his arms. "Honey, I should have known the heat would—"

She tore herself from him. "This was a stupid idea! Just stay away from me."

His expression darkened. "I'm not going to let you do this. You said—"

What she told him to do with her earlier comment was as much a physical impossibility as doing it with her seemed to be, but her earthy crack broke Adam's rising tension. He fought his laughter for a split second, but it burst from him. "I love to rile you up, Goddess. You're so much fun!"

Diana glared at him, blushing at her own words. "You're insane, aren't you? The men in the white coats are going to clear you out of here any minute."

"Oh, Diana, you surprise me at every turn. You're so full of spice, I think I might burn my tongue next time I kiss you."

"Don't do it, Yankee. You might not survive next time." The thought choked her. "Please stop trying."

But he merely shook his head. "You've never been a quitter before, Diana. Don't start now."

Her nostrils flared. "I am not a quitter!"

"Then you're stuck with me for the duration."

Stubbornly, she lowered her gaze. "You'll give up."

"No, Goddess, I won't. This isn't the last time. We will make love, I promise you, if it takes a week, or a month, I'm not going to give up." He turned her face up with a fingertip. "I promise," he repeated firmly. When she pulled away, he sighed. "What we need is a different setting."

"What we need is a miracle," she said, her voice trembling.

"No," he murmured. "Maybe we just need a bigger dose of magic to sweeten the pot."

"I don't believe in—" He cut her off with his mouth again, but didn't linger, to her secret chagrin.

"Don't think about it, just let it happen. I'll figure out something."

Without another word, he limped into the kitchen, whistling a cheerful tune.

Diana shook her head sharply. "What are you doing?"

"Dinner." He flourished a pot holder. "I filleted the bluegill and heated Weena's biscuits and washed and peeled those other things. Sit down, my shy little rabbit, and let me feed you for a change."

His rapid switch in mood baffled her, as usual, leaving her floundering. "But what about—"

"No more seduction tonight, only good food and talk of Ev and Weena." He grinned at her, something fierce lighting his blue eyes. "I'll take care of everything."

He wasn't a quitter, huh? Well, he sure backed off in a hurry! And it wouldn't be the last time, of that she was convinced.

Diana sat at the table, numbly watching as Adam suddenly was transformed into a mad scientist, even letting Dodger out of the stillroom to join in his antics as the trusted assistant, Igor. She and the cat both eyed Adam warily the rest of the evening, but even after he'd fixed her bed and cleared away the hanging sheets, he didn't drop the act. "Sleep well, my pretty," he chortled as he tucked her in despite her objections. "You'll need it."

His sudden, maniacal laughter echoed through the cabin, sending shivers over her.

Long after she had dropped into slumber like a rock into a deep pool, long after the fire had died to dull ash, Adam knelt beside Diana and gently brushed a strand of bright hair from her forehead. Well, he thought, at least his experiment in fantasy had proven one thing tonight—Diana wasn't afraid of sex. He had felt her surrender, had sensed her body's willingness, if not her mind's. One of many questions had been answered, and he counted it a triumph. Patience had never been one of his virtues; it was time to cultivate it. Life had taught him that dreams never came true, but he was beginning to realize he'd given up too easily, and maybe even sabotaged himself in the process. The future might be exactly as he imagined, if he made it so.

She believed him shallow and uncaring, and he'd thrown her for a loop today, which was exactly what she needed. Though he hadn't solved the mystery of Diana Machlen—yet—he knew that she suppressed a part of herself for reasons he didn't understand. All he had to do was keep her off balance, let her believe one thing with her practical little mind, then allow her distinctly *im*practical side to toss her on her beautiful bottom. He was on the right track with the fantasies, he thought, her reaction had proven that. But he'd have to time the next one perfectly.

"I love you," he whispered tenderly, knowing she couldn't hear him.

She shifted in her sleep and murmured something that sounded like, "Sweet dreams," then slept on, a tiny half-frown at her brow.

His smile wavered. "The sweetest," he told her, then kissed the frown away and limped to his empty bed.

Seven

When Adam awoke the next morning, dim light filtered through the window. He pulled himself out of bed and hobbled, shivering, to the bathroom. Afterward, Dodger greeted him with his usual nip on the ankle. "You love me, don't you?" Adam murmured.

Dodger gave him a scratch for good measure, then bounded away to "ack" at a cabinet. Inside, Adam found kibble, and poured a bowlful for him. The cat jumped in with both feet, growling his broken, snorting growl, as if to scare away food thieves.

Adam stared at him a moment, then shook his head and glanced out the window. No Snow White sat on the stump today.

He sighed, remembering his vow. Keep her off balance and get answers to his questions, huh? How could he do that when she kept disappearing at dawn? His eyes narrowed.

"You won't escape me that easily," he muttered. He quickly returned to his room and picked up his lucky jeans. No stains marred its pockets, but the frayed holes remained. Shrugging, Adam decided he needed them more than he needed the comfort his sweatpants provided, and struggled into them. Though tight against his bandage, they didn't hurt him. He slipped into his shoes, white T-shirt, and his bomber jacket, then limped stiffly past Dodger, who was amusing himself with an endless round of tail-chasing, and out into the chill morning air.

His breath made foggy clouds in the receding night as he walked behind the cabin. The single bird began its predawn chirping. Something skittered behind a bare-branched tree as his sneakers crunched over dead leaves and twigs. At the stump, he turned and headed through the bushes, in the direction from which Diana had come before.

Beyond the break, he found a faint trail and followed it through the trees. As he walked, tiny white flowers began to appear around the trunks, then blades of grass. A small snake, a bright, almost fluorescent green, slithered across his path. Branches budded, then blossomed into new leaves and fragile pink blooms. Somewhere to his left, he heard the faint babble of water over stones. It was as if Diana's cabin were locked in perpetual winter, while the rest of the world burst with new life.

Adam smiled grimly. Diana Machlen was, in truth, the Ice Queen, he thought. But he would bring spring to her. He simply loved her too much not to.

The forest ended quite abruptly. Adam halted, transfixed by the sight before him. A sea of colorful wildflower buds rippled gently in the early breeze, accentuated by the shadowed backdrop of rolling hills. And in the center of it all, knee-deep in the purples and yellows and blues, stood Diana. Dressed in a bulky green sweater and jeans, her wavy hair was unbound again and cascaded down her back in a stream of living flame. The pale light touched her softly with its rosy glow as she waded through the clearing, stooping occasionally to choose something for the basket over her arm.

He drew a ragged breath, wiped suddenly clammy palms down his pants, and limped forward.

"Good morning," he called out, wincing as his overly hearty greeting rebounded back. Several creatures rustled away from him as the tall plants bent beneath his feet and the dew wet his jeans. "Flowers for breakfast, hon?"

Diana's head snapped up at his words, and she froze in a crouch, like a wary animal catching an enemy's scent. "What are you doing here?" she asked.

"I had no one to talk to." He put on his best plaintive expression as he neared. "Dodger was quite content with his tail. Besides, he's not much of a conversationalist. He just says 'ack.' "

"His larynx was damaged, after a fight with a coyote, I think. I found him that way."

"So what's your excuse? I've never had a woman fall asleep on me before. Over and over!" He cocked his head. "Maybe that's the solution."

"What? Narcolepsy?

"No." He grinned. "You could treat me like a real husband."

She gasped. "In a pig's eye!"

"Sure, why not? I could drink beer and spill food all over the house. You could cook and clean and fetch and—"

"You want a maid, not a wife."

"Nah, this is cheaper. I quit my job, remember?" Despite his teasing tone, Adam found himself enjoying the thought of Diana as his wife. That didn't shock him as much as he thought it would. Well, not quite as much. "Maybe you'd even fall in love with me."

"When pigs fly."

"What is this fascination you have with porcine curses?"

Her eyes narrowed. "Are you ever serious?"

He frowned. "Once. I think."

"Adam, just go home. Leave me alone."

"I can't leave, Goddess. Not while I feel like I'm sitting on a Peace rose."

"You can't play on that injury forever, Adam. Be warned." Despite her words, she relaxed her pose. "Admit it. You just can't stand to be alone."

"*Moi*? I've been alone most of my life, Goddess, even in the middle of a crowded room. I'm the champion loner."

Diana opened her mouth to make an acid comment, but his undercurrent of bitterness, of old pain, stopped her cold. She'd sensed the tears beneath the clown before, and she'd always managed to ignore them. But it was becoming more difficult, she realized. The beast within her purred.

To cover her confusion, she snatched a random handful of flowers and yanked them from the ground. "I have research to do, things to—to gather. Go be alone."

"Last night, you weren't so standoffish, love. Last night, you melted in my arms."

She flushed. "Last night, you almost melted in your burnoose."

"So? You said it yourself, I'm hardheaded. I'm not going to give up. Are you?"

Her stomach clenched, and she couldn't speak.

He smiled lopsidedly and kissed her quickly on the mouth, then cocked his head. "You like to think you're so secretive, you know, but you're not. I know why you're out here, Goddess."

"You do?" she squeaked.

"Sure." His voice lowered to an ominous whisper. "I think you come out here at dawn to search for fairies."

She blinked. "Adam—"

"That's why you gambol in the dew, Goddess." He nodded firmly, his eyes twinkling. "Yep. You know their secrets, and you don't want the rest of the world to find out. I freaked when I read Tolkien, and I spent a whole summer searching for Hobbits too."

Diana swallowed hard, her vision suddenly blurring. He *knew*. He had seen her panic, and by changing the subject he had diffused it, as he had frequently done before. Was this Adam's version of compassion? Or was his humor a shield too? Who was protecting whom?

A raccoon chittered in the trees behind her. "I have to go," she whispered, dropping her gaze. "It's almost dawn."

"Back to the stump?"

"No, not today." She stifled her whirling emotions, babbling in the effort. "Crockett's heading for the stream, not the house, thank goodness. The last time he and his mate visited the cabin unattended, I lost most of a month's baking. Heaven help me if they make it in someday."

"Crockett?"

"The raccoon."

"Is his mate Tubbs?"

She looked at him blankly.

"*Miami Vice?*"

"Oh, TV. No, he's Davy."

He barked a short laugh. "And I thought *I* didn't make sense!"

"It makes perfect sense. Everything makes sense if you look close enough."

"You love this place, don't you?"

She nodded, warily watching him for any foaming at the mouth.

"Why?"

She frowned. "Do you really want to know?" At his nod, her frown deepened. He was so odd! "I guess part of it is because when the Rockies were infants, the Ozarks were already old men. The diversity of plant and animal life is amazing. Only the Appalachians can equal it."

"Very nice," he said. "Nice textbook explanation." His voice lowered. "You want to know something? It gets in my blood too."

Puzzled, Diana couldn't think of an answer, but the faraway chittering saved her from one. "I have to go."

"The raccoons again, huh?"

"Didn't you hear him?"

"I'm not as attuned to the place as you are, Goddess. Not yet, anyway."

His words implied more than she was willing to acknowledge right now, and she turned from him. "I'll meet you back at the cabin."

"I'd like to come with you."

She shook her head quickly. "The animals are used to my scent." She forced a smile. "And your footsteps have all the delicacy of a pregnant ox."

"Cow."

She opened her mouth, then closed it. "Beg pardon?"

"An ox is a neutered male, isn't it? Or was that deliberate?"

She shook herself. "Whatever. You'd still scare them off. Besides, you shouldn't be walking this far yet, Adam, and you definitely shouldn't be tramping about with no boots. You'll catch your death. And we have lots of critters who would love to make a meal of you."

"Like you?"

Startled, she met his gaze. He stood so close that she could see his bristly morning beard, smell her soap on his skin, the leather of his jacket. "Yes," she whispered involuntarily.

"Good. That's what I wanted to hear. A little honesty."

She frowned. "Just 'good'? No crack, no reflexive pounce?"

"Disappointed?" he asked with a grin.

Something inside her roared "Yes!" with a ferocity that made her quiver. "I figured that after last night, you'd think I was fair game."

"No, Goddess. No matter what happens, never that." He reached out to gently take the flowers from her hand. "I do need to know something, though."

She shook herself and took them back. "What?"

"What happened to Kyle?"

Her heartbeat went into overdrive. Her hand trembled so hard the flowers fell to the ground in a tangle. "He, uh . . ." She cleared her throat and forced a sweet smile. "He laughed at me, so I shot him."

Adam barked a laugh. "You made a joke, Goddess!"

"Are you sure?" she asked.

His chuckles subsided, his blue eyes warmed her. "Don't try to scare me with your Rambo tactics. You wouldn't hurt a flea purposely." His finger trailed over her jaw. "What happened?"

Mesmerized, she groped for another acid comment, but her breath caught in her chest. "I don't—" Her gaze dropped. She felt as knotted as the bouquet.

"Goddess?"

She wrestled with herself, but it was a losing battle. "He left me," she whispered finally. Before he could comment, she shoved the filled basket into his hands. "Would you take this back, please? Thanks." She strode away without a backward glance.

Adam stood staring after her until she glided into the thick forest brake, his heart twisting at her simple confession. He was making progress, but not enough.

Not a single snapping twig sounded at her passing. He frowned, looking from the growing light over the ridge to the path to the cabin, and back to her direction. Beneath the swelling birdsong, he heard the sound of water. Why was she so anxious to keep him away? It was as if she recharged in the morning, and she escaped from him into it. What significance did the dawn actually hold for her?

Adam didn't mind being alone, but he hated feeling excluded, and that was something Diana had better learn. "A pregnant ox, huh?" he muttered, and set the basket down. "Let's see what you're hiding, Goddess."

His limp prevented an accurate imitation of her noiseless glide, but Adam watched the forest floor carefully and managed to avoid most of the deadwood and leaves. While not entirely silent, the small rustles and cracks of his movements were muffled by the sheer density of trees. The sound of the creek guided him a short distance, to a place where the branches hung low, and roots were exposed on its banks. Bushes stood sentinels at the edge of the water. He ducked quickly behind one as he caught a flash of Diana's bright hair a little downstream. He winced as the reflex action pulled at his injuries, but he refused to be stymied. He wanted to see what was so important to her.

Slipping sideways into the brush, he leaned on his hands to take most of the weight off his bum leg, and edged toward her. As his cover ran out, he stopped. Diana was now clearly in view, and something told him not to alert her to his presence.

She sat cross-legged atop a low ridge above the stream, patiently unmoving. She frowned once, then shook her head and stared, her gaze riveted on the dimpled brown pool a bend in the creek had formed. A small beach, bracken scattered along it, indicated a previous, higher watermark. The raccoon she had heard earlier crouched at the bank, turning an egg over and over in the pool, obviously washing it. Facing him, a deer, her legs sprawled out, her sides bulging with an unborn fawn, flicked her long ears briefly in Adam's direction before lowering her head to drink again. Behind her, Adam caught a glimpse of the antlers of her mate, guarding his lady's safety. A sinuous gray creature undulated from the driftwood to bury its muzzle in the water. Birds fluttered down to splash. A mouse crept in for a quick drink before darting away. And to his astonishment, a coyote slinked in, so close he could see the black hairs among the tawny, then left without a second glance at his natural prey.

Adam remembered something about the watering holes in Africa, that they were places where no hunter and hunted existed, places where for a brief moment in time the animals declared a truce. But he never dreamed it was actually true.

He looked toward Diana. A tiny smile curved

her mouth. To his surprise, tears burned his eyes, a lump formed in his throat. Diana Machlen didn't believe in fairies, but she had her own special brand of magic, and she believed it more than she knew. Not only did she choose a place of truce, but instinctively she had chosen a time of great power, a time when the night and day came together, when the nocturnal and the diurnal both prowled the earth. Didn't she realize what was happening? Why did she deny it so vehemently when her actions proved otherwise? Her research involved plants, not animals, yet every morning she communed with them on a level that most people would think impossible, blithely wading in with predator and prey. He realized that absolutely no fear had ever crossed her face, at least out there. He wondered if it ever did.

Her expression changed abruptly to one of amusement. Adam glanced back toward the stream. All of the animals were warily edging away from something that rustled in the brush, and his heart lurched at the thought of what it might contain. But in a moment, he understood their caution. A small black-and-white-striped creature strode forward with the confidence of a crowned prince, its plumed tail high. Oblivious to the unblinking stares of the other animals, the skunk boldly took his place at the edge of the water, and Adam stifled a chuckle at the creature's audacity.

Wanting to share the joke, he began to stand, to join Diana despite the anger he knew she'd feel at his intrusion. But another sound, familiar but somehow out of place, made him freeze. It was a snuffly kind of grunt, and the doe jerked her head up, her ears rigid, then lumbered away. The others crouched in the same kind of posture he'd seen in Diana, except for the skunk, who calmly continued drinking.

Adam gulped and looked at Diana. She sat straight, her violet eyes as big as saucers, her body stiff. Her skin paled. His gaze snapped back toward the opposite bank as the branches of a low bush began to rustle, and from it poked a glistening snubbed nose. Slowly, the rest of a black head shoved through, then a huge, shaggy body ambled out on all fours, and he found himself staring at something he hadn't even know existed here. A bear!

His pulse raced as it moved closer and closer to Diana, but she didn't move! His mouth went dry. Lord, she was scared to death!

Without thinking twice, Adam groped for a weapon. His hand closed around a large stick. He raised it and charged from his cover, forgetting another, more imposing danger in his rush to protect Diana.

The creature turned and fired.

"I didn't touch you, so don't you dare try and blame yourself."

"I'm not blaming myself, Adam. I told you that before."

"I was only trying to protect you."

"I figured that out."

"I didn't think about the skunk."

"I'm certain you didn't," Diana said blandly, pinching her lips tight. Wrinkling her nose, she concentrated on the shortcut through the forest, never once glancing behind to see if he kept up with her quick pace. She didn't have to. She could tell without looking that he was far too close for comfort. Her nostrils burned from the heavy musk.

"Could you move to your left, please? The wind shifted again."

"This makes no sense at all. I'm the kind of person who catches taxis in the rain in the middle of rush hour in New York City! Buses *never* pull away from the curb before I get there. I had four job offers before I even resigned, did you know that?"

"No, Adam," she said patiently, stifling a smile. "You've told me about your luck with cars, women, and taxis a hundred times in the last ten minutes, but that's a new one. Were they better jobs?"

"Not necessarily." He sighed. "Okay, maybe I've screwed up a few things in my life. Maybe I expect too much sometimes. I understand that. But I prepared for you, I didn't set myself up. Well, not really. So why is everything going wrong? And don't say a word about your blasted jinx! This one had nothing to do with you!"

"Do you always babble in times of crisis?" she asked, wondering what in the hell he was talking about.

"Yes. It's safer than punching someone's lights out. I'm a physical coward, Diana, I think you should know that before you fall in love with me."

A giggle bubbled in her throat. She pretended a nasty cough. "And like the wimp you are, you went after a bear with a hunk of wood."

"I pretended it was a baseball bat and the bear was this really obnoxious umpire I used to know. Same stupid expression and cross-eyed glare. How was I supposed to know he had a pint-sized bodyguard?" he groaned. "It's not fair. The only time I ever play hero, and I'm ground into dust by a mutant rodent."

Wiping the grin from her face, she peeped over her shoulder. Adam plodded along behind, his eyes streaming against the odor that rose from him. The white of the bandage on his forehead stood out starkly against his flushed skin. "If it's any consolation, you terrified that poor bear. They're really quite gentle, and rarely attack humans."

"Now, you tell me!"

"You never gave me a chance. I didn't ask you to follow me."

He glared at her. "I thought you were scared of it."

"It takes a lot more than a single bear, groggy from hibernation, to scare me."

"What were you planning to do? Light a fire and keep him at bay?"

"I could have outrun that lazybones in nothing flat."

"Thank you *so* much for telling me this was a wasted effort. Couldn't you simply lie and say you were frightened?"

She chose the right fork of the path through the woods, toward her cabin. "I was excited, if you must know. Black bears are rare here, now. It's only in the last ten or fifteen years that they've been reintroduced, and the balance—"

"You know what? I don't care about the damned bear anymore! If I never hear another word about their habitat or dietary requirements or their place in the food chain, it will be too soon. And don't you try to tell me that this is the skunk's reflex action because I startled him. I already know that. And I don't care. I still reek."

"Actually, you got off easy. Skunks aim for the face. If you hadn't stood—"

"Diana," he said with a growl, "don't push it." He stomped in syncopated silence for a while.

"What would you have done if he had been vicious?" he asked softly.

"He wasn't."

"No, Goddess, I mean it. You don't take your shotgun with you in the morning, and you've lived in the middle of nowhere for years, all by yourself. What happens in a real emergency? Good Lord, woman, you could lie in a ditch for weeks before anyone found you!"

"Oh, for—" She sighed, hating the guilt she felt over his anxiety. She despised being fluttered over. It was one of the side effects of a large and too-close family. "Don't worry about me, all right? I haven't had so much as a cold in all the time I've been here." She heard him draw a breath, and anticipated him. "I neither want nor need a phone. Everybody around here looks out for one another." She patted her pocket. "I have keys to at least eight houses in the area. During my morning rounds, I check up on them."

"That's not very reassuring."

"Adam, I visit my friends over the hill twice a week. If I don't show up, they come looking for me." She checked the angle of the sun, impatient with explanation. "In fact, if I don't get going soon, I'll have a posse after me."

"Why don't you just go?" he said tightly. "I'll manage."

"I know the routine, you don't. I can at least get it out of your skin, but I don't think your jeans—" She cut herself off and nearly slapped herself for triggering the endless lament he'd given at the creek.

"My jeans," he said, moaning. "These are my lucky jeans."

Diana turned to him in exasperation. "For pity's sake, Adam! They're just a piece of denim sewn into two tubes and connected at the crotch, not holy relics!"

He strode up to her. "Look, lady, I've never had many things in my life that I care about, and certainly few possessions that were mine alone, but these jeans and my car and a couple of other items have more value than you could ever imagine!"

Her heart ached for him, but she coughed as the stench reached her, and her sympathy took a nosedive. She straightened to her full five-feet-six and glared into his chin. "Not anymore, they don't."

His eyes narrowed. "No, no, no. You're not throwing these out!"

"They have holes from the shot, and now—"

"Over my dead body," he told her, then smiled to soften his emphatic words—or to prevent the obvious reply. "You're really quite brave, aren't you, wildcat?"

If he only knew, she thought sadly. "That's not courage you see, it's nausea."

"You are a little green around the gills."

Her nostrils quivered, and she covered her nose as she backed a step. "It's your cologne, Mr. Daniels. I think you got gypped."

"Oh, I don't know." He sniffed, waving his hand as if mulling over the bouquet of a rare wine. "Subtle yet heavy, impertinent yet pervasive. It makes a statement."

"Sure. 'City dump.'" She relented when she saw his woebegone expression. How could she stay angry—or poke fun at—a man who looked like an extra in *Rambo* and acted as if this kind of mutilation happened every day? No matter the outcome, he had tried to save her life. Her conscience stung with things she'd thought about him, he heart ached with emotions she couldn't begin to sort through. "Adam, I . . ." She trailed off and leapt for the clearer air. This was hardly the time for maudlin gratitude, or anything else! "I'm sorry, I can't take it anymore! You need fumigation!"

"Goddess—"

The walls of her cabin peeked through the trees just in front of her, and she hurried to arrive before Adam. She didn't want that scent in her house one moment longer than absolutely necessary, so she'd have to get a jump on him. "Go straight to the bathroom and undress!" she called over her shoulder. "I'll be waiting!"

"Is this a proposition?"

"It's self-preservation! If I have to strip every inch of your skin with my fingernails, I will!"

Adam watched her disappear around the corner of her cabin, and halted in the middle of the path, exhaling slowly, puffing his cheeks. Why had fate chosen this woman? She was trying to murder him, he thought reasonably. His backside ached, his nose rebelled against the stench of his body, and his chest heaved with the effort of trying to keep up with her. The rising sun had warmed the temperature, heating the obnoxious scent and beading his brow with sweat. He winced at the mixture, realizing he smelled like the bad end of a camel.

Rolling his gaze heavenward, he wondered if someone up there was silently laughing His head off. His bandage unstuck and flopped over his eye. With a sigh, he peeled it off and absently stuffed it into his pocket. If he were a superstitious man, he decided as he forged ahead, he could almost believe Diana wasn't the only one who was jinxed. They certainly batted a thousand together. "Makes sense," he muttered with a nod. "She causes disasters when she's aroused, and I cause them when she appeals to something *other* than my libido." He raised his hands to the sky. "At this rate, we'll never get together!" he shouted.

"Good," came the faint reply.

Squelching an instinctive riposte, he drew a deep, bracing breath. Fine. His demise would be on her head. Either he would explode from desire or burst from frustration, or he would bleed to death from injuries sustained in the weirdest battle of wills he had ever fought. One way or another, it seemed, Diana Machlen would put him in his grave.

He hitched up his pants and squared his shoulders. Everything that could go wrong had already, so what more did he have to lose? If he had to die he would do it with a smile on his face. Even if it killed him.

He unsnapped his jeans, unzipped his jacket, and hobbled toward certain doom.

Eight

Diana raced around the cabin, flinging open windows. Dodger watched her with typical feline curiosity, his ears perked forward, until she made a grab for him. Obviously knowing she planned to lock him up somewhere, he bolted under the sofa, and Diana decided she didn't have time to chase him. If he made it outside, he'd probably just entrench himself beneath the porch anyway. Adam was her main concern now.

She opened the closet and gathered all of her towels. After dumping them on the toilet seat, she twisted the bathtub taps and returned to the kitchen to check her supply of tomato juice. One quart, she saw, which was hardly enough. She frowned, mentally ticking off alternatives. There was one possibility, but she hadn't tested it yet. Sighing, she realized she had no choice, and shoved up her sweater's sleeves.

Behind her, Dodger hissed. She darted a quick look over her shoulder. He skittered away from the front door, his back arched and every black hair standing straight up. Her gaze flew to the cause of the commotion, and she swallowed hard. Adam stood in the doorway, leaning against the jamb, the sunlight from the widow above her illuminating every inch of his magnificent body. Strong, lean, and wiry, like a dark jungle predator, Adam Daniels was so blatantly male, he nearly stopped her heart.

And he wore nothing but a wicked grin.

"*Chérie*," he murmured, raising a single brow. "I have arrived."

She dropped her gaze, but she zeroed in on the shadow between his thighs. Her eyes widened. Heat flushed her face, her ears burned. "Why don't you go stand in the tub?" she managed to rasp out, jerking her thoughts—and her head—back up. It took a moment for her gaze to follow. *Skating rink*, she thought automatically, but that trick didn't seem to work very well anymore.

His regard intensified, flaring with dark fire as he loped toward her. "You're not very good at hiding your emotions, are you, Goddess?" he whispered.

Now she knew how a rabbit felt when it saw the headlights, she thought dazedly. "Adam, I—" His overpowering musk reached her nostrils, destroying her building desire more effectively than her frigid images ever had. Thank heavens, she thought. Nothing happened this time.

Shuddering, she stood, trying desperately to breathe as little as possible. "I have to get something."

He snatched her hand, his intensity fading in the wake of an exaggerated leer. "Oh, my darling," he crooned in a horrible French accent. "You must let me keess you."

She tried to pull away. "Adam, this isn't funny."

Despite her statement, the last word sputtered out like a snort. Nerves, she thought, and fought the heat that still radiated inside of her. "Stop before another shelf crashes to your head."

"It's worth the risk." He pressed his mouth to hers.

She tore herself from him before the wonderful sensation could take root. "I don't believe you! In case you hadn't noticed, the, uh, atmosphere isn't conducive to seduction."

"I am wounded, *chérie*. My aroma ees only that of love."

"Then I pray to die an old maid."

He kissed her wrist with a noisy smack. "Your beauty inspires me, you leetle veexen, you." With an elaborate moan, he worked his way up her arm. "Do not deny eet, do not fight our passion. I know I drive you mad."

Her eyes misted, retaliating against the fumes. "True, all true," she told him sweetly. "Now, let go of me before I throw up."

He peeked up at her from her elbow. "I am irresistible, no?"

"You are irresistible, no."

He pouted, but released her. "You have no humor, *chérie*. I am deesappointed."

"You and me both." Diana darted into the still-room and grabbed a bottle from the cluttered table. "Lord, I hope this works," she muttered. "Otherwise you'll have to sleep on the roof."

Adam's eyes widened. "Tell me you know what you're doing."

She smiled and took his elbow. "I know what I'm doing."

"This does not inspire me with confidence."

"Don't worry, Pépé," she choked, dragging him to the bathroom. "In several blinks of our abused eyes, you won't even notice it anymore."

Thirty minutes later, Diana sprinted to the porch, her lungs nearly bursting. Grasping the rail so tightly it cut into her hands, she drew great draughts of fresh, untainted air, chill from the sudden cloud cover. "It's getting nasty out here," she told him through the window. "The weather is quite unpredictable in the Ozarks."

"Diana," rumbled Adam from the bathroom, his tone restrained. "Stop avoiding the issue. You said this was the perfect solution."

"I'm sorry," she called. "I thought it would work."

"I'm going to tear you limb from limb, Diana."

"Nana's journal promised this would neutralize the musk!"

"I smell like a brothel, Diana."

Her lips quivered, and she covered her mouth to stifle waves of merriment. He wouldn't appreciate it right now. "Just give me a minute, okay?" she said, her voice trembling despite her best efforts. Back to plan A, she thought, and dashed back inside for the acidic juice. Her cabin reeked with the sickly sweet odor of Nana's "cure." "I'll fix it, Adam, I promise."

"That's what you said before, Diana."

She eyed the single quart in disgust, then, shrugging, snatched up three others containing various ingredients.

"Will you hurry, please?" His voice rose. "I think this stuff is eating my skin."

"Hold your water, Adam." She juggled the glass jars precariously into her arms.

"I'm serious, here. There's this little green patch on my knee, and it's spreading."

She burst through the door and set the jars down on the floor, barely glancing at Adam. In spite of the horrible scent, his body still had the power to rob her mind of rational thought if she let it. Was that the reason the de-skunker had had such dire consequences? "This'll work," she murmured, and opened the quart.

"I like mine *al dente*," he quipped.

"It's not spaghetti sauce, it's tomato juice."

"Great. Another home remedy?"

"It works."

"Why didn't you use it in the first place?"

"Because I don't really have enough." Without looking at his face, she poured the liquid all over his legs and scrubbed with a washcloth.

"Diana, I'm not sure I want to know, but what's in the other jars?"

She ignored him. "See? It's even covering up that patch on your knee."

"It's turning it brown."

"So you'll look like you have a great tan." When that jar was empty, she opened the next.

"Diana," he warned, stepping back slightly. "That's not juice."

"I know."

"This is really kinky."

"Just shut up, okay?" Before he could say another word, she smashed the first tomato into his hard thigh.

Afterward, Adam dressed in his gray sweatpants and shirt, limping to the main room, where he found Diana with her head buried in her journal, her hair already plaited. She glanced up once, her violet eyes twinkling, then returned to her writing. He sidled up to her and tugged on the trailing end of the braid. "Writing about the bear?"

"Yes. I'll have to report the sighting to the conservation department."

"I hope you don't put in the park about the skunk."

"Oh, I don't know. That was kind of the high point of the experience."

"Hold on, let me see that."

She closed the book with a clap. Their gazes locked, and she looked away first, stifling a smile. "You're none the worse for wear," she said in a shaky voice.

"Other than the fact that I smell like cheap room freshener," he said solemnly, "I think we did rather well."

She quickly cut hickory nut bread and smeared it with wild strawberry jam, thumping the plates to the table before she could laugh outright. Why she fought it, she didn't know, but she sensed that he would use it as another opening.

They ate in silence, Diana avoiding his direct gaze, but she felt his eyes on her. She shifted in her chair, glanced up, then shifted again. "What?" she asked finally. "Do I have seeds in my teeth or something?"

He sank his chin to his hand. "No. I was just wondering, with all your knowledge of folklore and everything . . ."

She eyed him warily. "Spit it out, Adam."

He crossed his arms over his broad chest and eased carefully back in his chair. "The more I know you, the more I'm beginning to believe you're as practical and down-to-earth as you told me. The germ of truth in the legends, and everything."

She waited. "And?"

"I just can't figure out why you're so superstitious."

"I'm not," she told him. "You're the one with the lucky jeans, not me, remember?"

He waved that away. "You're convinced you're jinxed. Isn't that on par with an omen?"

She shook her head and bit into her toast. "Two

totally different things. Oh, I'll admit omens tweak a bit of the primal mind. I don't know anyone who purposely breaks a mirror or walks under a ladder. But that doesn't mean they're necessarily superstitious. I think it's just a—a lingering psychological implication or something. It could be a self-fulfilling prophecy." She remembered the coffee ring, but it wasn't the same thing. Adam was far too attractive on his own. She needed no omen to tell her that. "They're not scientific," she finished firmly.

"I wonder." He continued to watch her for a moment, took a drink of milk, then smiled suddenly. "Let's try an experiment."

"What kind of experiment?" she asked, frowning. "Like the one you tried when the soup boiled over?"

"Not exactly. We've had a lot of bad luck lately, right?" He grinned. "Let's change it."

She gaped at him. "Just like that?"

"Sure, why not? Okay, help me out here. Give me some good-luck omens."

"You're crazy," she said in amazement.

"I know," he agreed solemnly. "But this is something we both want, right?"

"I assume so." She wondered at his reasons, but shook off the sudden doubt. "I know I do." She had to shush herself a second time for her own reasons. "But, Adam—"

"C'mon, love, don't let's defeat ourselves before we've started." His voice took on the quivering tenor of a professional orator. "We will beat the enemy on the land, the sea, and the air!"

"I think you want Winston Churchill, and you misquoted him."

He waved his hand. "I'm on a roll. This is a great idea! Why didn't I think of it before?" He stood and beckoned with his fingers. "Gimme."

Despite her practical objections, Diana chuckled. "All right. Um . . ." Her eyes narrowed. "Find a pin and pick it up, all day long you'll have good luck."

His gaze swept the room. "No pins. Try again."

She racked her brain. "Sleeping with your head toward the north brings good luck the next day."

He eyed her sofa, then her. "You already do."

"I do?" She glanced at it. "For pity's sake, I never noticed. A lot of good it's done me."

"Don't start. Okay, another."

She sighed, lowering her head to her hands. "Seeing a toad in the road, finding initials in a spider's web, dreaming about death, dropping a glass without breaking it—"

"That's it!" He emptied his milk glass and let it go. It crashed to the floor.

"Adam!"

Undaunted, he reached for hers and repeated the performance. It broke too. He sighed and limped to her cabinet.

"Wait!" she cried, knowing he'd probably destroy her entire supply if she let him. Her adrenaline surged with sudden urgency. "Uh, a four-leafed clover, a horseshoe over the doorway, a"—she clenched her fists—"a falling star, seeing a white cat on the road when traveling . . ." She paused, running out of omens. When he grabbed the flour canister from the counter and turned with a wicked glint in his blue eyes, she gasped, a giggle bubbling to the surface. "Adam, you can't be serious."

He grinned and crouched, tilting his head to see beneath the sofa. "Oh, Dodger. How about a little trip?"

She leapt to her feet. "I have it! When—when you're experiencing bad luck, walk around a chair three times to make it good."

He straightened. "That's it?"

She dropped back to her chair. "That's it."

"Seems kind of anticlimactic, doesn't it?"

She shrugged. "It's the best I can do."

"Okay." He hobbled around his chair three times. "Now you."

Feeling foolish, she did it too. "Now what?"

"Now, we wait." He grabbed her broom and swept the glass into a neat pile.

"How long?"

"As long as it takes."

She nodded and stood. She should have known this would go nowhere. "Maybe I should get the rest of your clothes and the basket we left in the meadow."

He touched her shoulder. "And maybe you should wait right here."

She hastily cleared her throat. "Adam, I—"

Before she could finish, Dodger began keening. Diana's head tilted up, and she tensed. Oh, no, thought Adam, he wouldn't let her use this to her advantage this time! "Incoming cat!" he yelled, and dived to the floor, pulling her with him to avoid the glass.

She gasped, but instead of searing his ears with invectives, she began to giggle. Astonished, Adam hauled himself to his elbows and stared down into her face. She met his gaze for a moment, pressing her lips tightly together, but the frizzed-up Dodger sprang onto Adam, tangled with his hair, then darted away. Unable to control it any longer, she loosed the flood. Adam watched in wonder as it transformed her completely, enjoying each bubble of amusement as a rare and precious jewel.

His goddess of fire was a constant surprise to him, he thought. And he would have her, no matter how many times he had to suffer with her supposed jinx, no matter how many fantasies he had to create, no matter how many injuries he endured. She was worth everything.

When her laughter subsided to a mere trickle, he brushed a fringe of hair from her temple, a stray tear from her cheek. "It wasn't that funny," he said with a grin. But his heart swelled anyway.

She shook her head. "I know. I don't know what happened."

"Do you realize it's the first time I've heard you laugh, Goddess? Really laugh?"

Her smile softened. "I guess so," she murmured. "I—I've wanted to, but—" She glanced away. "I don't understand why you're still around."

"Don't you?"

Diana didn't want to see the intensity of his eyes, she wanted to block out the warmth of his body as it pressed against her side, but she couldn't quite ignore it.

Before another disaster could crash down around their heads, she sighed. "I don't know what I think anymore." She rolled from beneath him and rose, then turned to give him a hand up.

He took it, heaved himself to his feet, but didn't release her. "Admit it," he said softly. "You like me."

She opened her mouth, lowered her gaze, and nodded.

"Good. Maybe the luck is kicking in already." He squeezed her hand briefly and let it go. He didn't want to push his advantage. "Dodger disappeared into the bathroom," he said. "I'll try to find him."

"Look under the porch. He gets out through the window, but he never goes far. I'll go get our things." She started out the door, then returned to lock up her journal, which she'd left on the table.

He made no comment, but watched her with his crooked smile until she headed out again. "Are you coming back?"

She nodded. "I'll be home for lunch." She bolted for the door again.

"Meet me in the meadow!" he called. "We'll have a picnic."

"Great," she said, quelling her hope. Her stomach suddenly felt as though it held a ton of rocks, but her steps had a lightness she couldn't hide.

Diana hurried through her brief rounds around the neighborhood, reporting the bear from Weena's telephone. Her friend cackled over Adam's problem with the skunk, and her raisin-brown eyes had a subtle twinkle Diana didn't understand. But she found herself not wishing to waste precious minutes in gossip, and ran out the door.

She raced through her foraging, absentmindedly jerking a handful of totally inconsequential plants from the ground before she noticed. Every time she checked her watch, the hours seemed to crawl slower and slower with a pace that would make any tortoise proud. When the hands finally reached the appointed hour, she flew down the familiar path, suspecting Adam's intent. He'd already hit one of her fantasies right on the money; could he have figured out another?

When she burst from the forest, she saw her suspicions were correct. A raven-haired Roman demigod sprawled on one of her blankets, surrounded by nodding wildflowers. The toga he wore barely covered anything at all, and his classically handsome features fit the role to perfection. Now, she could understand how Jupiter had seduced all those poor mortal women.

How did he know?

Her steps faltered at the thought, but she shook herself and continued on, telling herself Adam wouldn't stoop so low as to read her journals. They had been safely locked up, and he hadn't asked questions she didn't want to answer. He didn't want that intimacy any more than she did, he had proven that over and over. His outrageous solution to her jinx, that she would fall in love with him, was an expedient answer for him. But she had to admit he did a good job in the attempt. She just had unoriginal fantasies, that was all, and if Adam knew anything, he knew women.

"Peel you a grape?" he asked with a naughty smile.

Her heart pounded, but she fought for a light tone as she sat at the edge of the blanket. Why, when she'd admitted she liked him, did she suddenly feel awkward and snappy? "I don't see any grapes."

"Ah, you must use your overactive little imagination, woman." He held up a jar full of something purple. "I'm a master of improvisation."

She raised her gaze to the cottony gray sky. "For someone who is a master, you sure picked a lousy day for a picnic."

He waved away her comment. "It wouldn't dare. I'm in charge of that department, remember? Besides, those aren't storm clouds, it's just a bit of haze. It's very warm today, at least out here."

"Adam—"

"Are you going to make excuses, or are you going to enjoy yourself?"

She sighed. "I just don't want to get wet."

"Actually, that has definite appeal."

"You have the bawdiest mind I've ever known." Despite herself, she smiled.

"I'll take that as a compliment. Now relax."

She hesitated, then plopped to the blanket. Once there, she twiddled with a flower, looking at everything but his bare legs and torso. Though she knew it was her rampant imagination, or some bizarre combination of the "cure" and the musk, she swore she smelled chocolate. "Do you really think walking around a chair will make a difference?"

"There's only one way to find out." Slowly, he dipped a finger into the gooey jam and slid it into his mouth. "Delicious."

Her pulse began to race. "I don't have any biscuits."

"Who needs them? This is much better." He repeated his sensual movement, his gaze holding hers. "Would you like some?"

"No," she said tersely. He did it again, and she couldn't help but watch his finger as it slowly caressed his lips, disappearing over and over as he pulled it out and sucked it in, laving off every drop of jam. Her tongue darted out to moisten her lips, almost tasting the tart wild grapes on herself. His eyes darkened, and he followed the path of her tongue with another sticky fingerful. Diana began to lick it off, but he shook his head and leaned forward, traveling the trail himself.

Warmth exploded through her as he licked her lips, the sensation so erotic and intimate, she wanted to groan aloud. When his hand touched her breast, she jumped, but he invaded her mouth with the same gentle ruthlessness he had shown before, dizzying her.

Something cold stabbed her forehead, then another drop fell on her nose. Her eyes flew open. "Adam," she said against his mouth.

"Shh," he told her, feeding her another bit.

Automatically, she took his finger in her mouth. Icy droplets pattered her head, her shoulders. "It's raining."

"So? What's a little rain?"

He kissed her again, silencing her objections.

"It didn't work."

"So?"

"I'm sorry."

"Dod't start agaid, Diada. You cad't tell be you dew it was goig to—to—" Adam stifled another sneeze to get the last word out. "Sleet!"

Wordlessly, she filled the pan at his feet with warm water, her shoulders slumped. "You believe me now, don't you? I'm jinxed."

Adam shivered. He was beginning to, but he wouldn't admit that to her or himself. "Baybe it takes a while for the luck to kick id."

"No, it's just me. Please don't try another, Adam, or you might end up with pneumonia."

Her defeat twinged his heart. "I thi'k it was fud."

"Fun!" Her eyes narrowed. "You had absolutely no protection. You could have been naked for all that toga did for you."

"Serves be right," he muttered with a grin, and huddled into the blanket.

She slammed the kettle to the floor. "Yes, by heaven, it does!"

With that, she stomped into the bathroom. Adam chuckled to himself. He sneezed violently and groped for the tissue box. This was merely another temporary setback, he told himself. By evening, his head would be clear if he had to take every nasty medicine known to man. Even sick, his body throbbed with unfulfilled desires, and if he didn't do something about it soon, he really would go insane!

He stared into the fire, thinking, then headed to his room when she didn't return. The place had been perfect, he had seen it written all over her face. But something had been missing. Diana might say she wanted him as much as he wanted her, but so far she hadn't given any indication that any inner truce had been declared.

"If this is the war of the sexes," Adam muttered as he crawled into bed, "I think I've bore thad earned by Purple Heart." He turned on his side, the evidence of past defeats twinging. If things didn't get better soon, he might just believe in her jinx. Maybe he'd have better luck being himself. At least for a while.

The thought almost frightened him as he drifted off to sleep.

Nine

The next day, Diana was as bristly as ever, and Adam cursed his lousy timing of the second fantasy. He'd jumped the gun, dammit, but he was determined to be absolutely certain for the next one, as soon as he figured out what it would be.

Dodger zoomed around the cabin after Diana had made her morning journal entry, and after they spent nearly an hour coaxing him from beneath the porch, Adam vowed to fix the escape route. Diana frowned at his sudden turnaround and hurried off.

When she returned hours later, she found Adam standing beneath the broken bathroom window, muttering about spring-loaded cranks or something equally Greek to her. "Don't worry," he told her. "I'll figure it out."

She fixed lunch, and he kissed her briefly in thanks, then went joyfully back to pull the window from its hinges. She shook her head. Adam bounced around more than Dodger. Wondering

134

where it all would end, she left for the rest of her foraging.

That night, her newly repaired window blocked even her best efforts to shove it open. Dodger "acked" at it, rebuking Adam, and avoided them all evening. Her thoughts whirling, Diana ate dinner, then prepared to take her bath. Remembering his original intent, for her to love him, she hesitated at the door. "Adam?"

"Yes, Goddess?"

"What happens if I do fall in love with you?" Her eyes widened. She hadn't meant to be so direct! "Hypothetically, of course."

He chuckled. "Hypothetically, what do you think will happen?"

"*Would* happen," she corrected firmly. She caressed the wooden jamb, absently picking at a splinter. "I think you'd puff up like Dodger. I think you'd gloat, and you'd be totally unbearable for weeks."

"No, Goddess," he whispered. "If you fell in love with me, I would think the moon, the stars, and the sun had come to rest in my pocket. I would think every perfect flower that had ever bloomed could not compare to the beauty you had given me. I believe my heart would swell to such proportions that no body on earth could contain it."

Her throat tightened with the intensity of his words. She lifted her gaze to him. "Hypothetically, of course," she said in a raspy voice.

One corner of his mouth lifted. "Of course."

Much to her private dismay, Adam made no overt moves on her the rest of the evening, but Diana went to sleep with a smile on her face.

After breakfast the next morning, he surprised her again with a wish to go with her into the fields. "I can't drive," he told her, "and I have to get out of here."

Confused, as usual, she frowned. "Four walls syndrome?"

He shrugged. "I lived in an orphanage until I was seven. I feel confined."

Diana realized she really didn't know him at all, and something clenched inside her, but he wouldn't let it rest. After nothing would induce Adam to stay home, she didn't protest again when he dogged her footsteps, except to point out that it didn't do his injuries any good.

"Nonsense," he told her firmly. "I need to stretch the muscles. All this forced inactivity is doing more harm than a little walking will do."

She grinned. "I won't say I told you so," she promised.

"Ha!"

As she suspected, their "little" walk caused Adam to fall face-first into his rabbit stew that night. "You do this every day?" he asked groggily as she helped him to bed.

"Of course not."

He brightened.

"Most of the time I go farther."

He collapsed to the mattress with a groan and fell instantly asleep.

To her surprise, he was just as determined the next morning. The day clouded over early, and they had to wear their jackets. But the rain never fell. In the afternoon, he followed her to Weena's, his steps lagging a bit when they neared the cottage. "What's wrong?" she asked. "Afraid they'll bite? Don't worry, Adam. They seem a little stand-offish at first sometimes, at least to strangers, but this area has some of the warmest people on earth."

He shrugged. "It's not them I'm worried about," he muttered.

Diana was baffled until they entered and Weena greeted Adam with a hug and a merry joke, both of which he returned. Ev, Weena's bespectacled husband, stepped up to shake his hand, then retreated to stand beside his wife. Diana glanced up at Adam, stunned by this familiarity. Damn, she knew Weena had been hiding something during her last visit! She bristled instinctively. "So you know each other."

"You're very territorial," he observed with raised brows. "My adoptive sisters were the same way. Do you want a rock?"

Remembering the scar on his mouth, she retreated. While she helped Weena with the housework, Adam climbed the apple tree to the roof and swept out the gutters, with Ev standing below to hand items up.

Silently, she dusted the high shelves in the pantry. Weena clomped up behind her with her walker, and Diana forced a smile to her face. "Have you been getting enough rest?" she asked.

Weena cackled. "Some. But ever since Adam showed up here, Ev's been spendin' more time to home. Jealous as a tick hound, that man."

"How long—" She cleared her throat and wiped off a can of peas. "I mean, I can't figure out when he—"

"Oh, he's popped in a couple of times. Never stays long, but helps out a bit, you know."

"That's Adam all over," she murmured.

After they finished there, they walked down the road to Matt's lodge, slinging their jackets over their shoulders as the sun finally made an appearance. Diana kept up a nonstop monologue about every plant and animal they passed until

Adam stopped her with a brief, unthreatening kiss.

"What was that for?" she asked breathlessly.

He shrugged. "It needed to be done. Relax, Goddess, I'm not going to pounce. Not yet, anyway."

That hardly reassured her, but she subsided in her lecture.

At the lodge, she checked to make sure Nathan was healthy and doing his usual work, then tracked down Matt to pass along a jar of Weena's homemade strawberry jam. He thanked her with typical lack of exuberance, his weathered face pulled down into his usual sad mask, then turned to eye Adam, who had stopped to gaze over the lake and now limped toward them. "Friend of yours?" he asked solemnly.

She nodded, and Matt greeted Adam with no hostility. They talked about the lodge for a moment, Adam asking why he was selling when the place seemed to be in such good shape.

"Gettin' too old," Matt told him. "And it'll only hold twenty or so, not much of a living." He shrugged. "Whatever I get, I'll bank, and move up with my sister in Phoenix." He eyed the clear sky and clicked his tongue. "Nasty as anything earlier. Prob'ly have a tornado tomorrow. Never know here'bouts. These bones can't take the temperamental weather around here much longer."

"You know," Adam said musingly, "you could draw tourists away from the north if the roads were a little better, or if you had an airstrip around here somewhere."

Matt shook his head dolefully. "Not worth it anymore."

They left soon afterward, and Diana glanced up at Adam, who walked beside her with a pensive frown. Her heart seemed to swell in her chest.

"You really wanted to help him, didn't you?" she whispered.

"Why wouldn't I?" he asked, obviously surprised at her question.

She just shook her head, wondering if she'd ever figure him out.

The next day, they wandered the hills, gathering nature's bounty, and this time Adam even asked questions. "Plantain," he said as she tugged the greens from the dirt, repeating her identification. "Our salads are Ozark weeds."

She chuckled, more of her reserve melting at his real interest. "One man's weeds . . ." she said airily. "Actually, it's not native to the area. The Indians here call it 'footsteps of the white man' because the settlers brought it, and it escaped the boundaries of their gardens." Her gaze drifted to the shadowed hills, a smile curving her mouth. "A lot of Ozark standards die out, but others take their places and naturalize themselves quickly."

"I could see why they'd want to," he murmured. "It's beautiful here." He cleared his throat roughly. "It sounds silly to say it, but I envy you. You have a place you belong. I never really had that." He glanced up at her, the wicked gleam back in his blue eyes. "Besides your bed, of course."

"So you say," she said, her voice trembling. Adam had his secrets too, it seemed. She almost wished she could share hers, to trade them and possibly diminish them in the process, but neither of them was very good at opening up. But his comment about belonging . . .

Confused by the sudden tenderness that sprang into her heart, Diana pushed on, telling him the uses for several of the plants they encountered, both according to legend and to fact. Sometimes he laughed over the old beliefs, but Diana told him that many of the so-called superstitions had proven out. Weather signs, planting times, many of them had a basis in fact, and the sayings and omens were simply ways to pass the information along and to remember it. To her surprise, she couldn't leave it at that, and found herself telling him about her upbringing on the small South Carolina island, even some of the "hoodoo" the Sea Islanders practiced.

"You grew up with such dark magic," he muttered under his breath. Before she could comment, Adam countered with some of the baseball superstitions he'd seen in his brief stint in the minors, some of which had her roaring with laughter.

As they returned to the cabin, she grew silent, embarrassed that she had divulged so much of herself. Once inside, Adam built a fire. It might have warmed up afield, but her cabin was still in the shadow of the bluff. She warmed herself beside the fire, then the stove as she cooked an early dinner. While they ate, Adam said very little, staring at her with a puzzled frown on his brow. It was the same problem-solving look she'd seen just before their good-luck episode, the same she'd seen at Matt's.

Diana shifted in her chair, glanced up, then shifted again. She cut into her succulent quail, but it tasted like ashes. "What?" she asked finally.

Adam sank his chin to his hand for a moment, then took a bite of his wild-rice stuffing. "You've closed up again, that's all. I thought . . ." He shook his head and finished his dinner.

Later that night, he wondered how he could keep fighting for her when she fought herself even harder. His eyes narrowed on the knothole beside his bed as he finally hit on the one way he could declare a truce.

And he smiled.

The next morning, Diana awoke with a start. The cabin was quiet—too quiet, as if the actual wake of a noise had left a gaping hole in the atmosphere. Obviously, she thought, something had awakened her, some sound, something out of place. But what?

The sun sent faint fingers of light into the room, telling her she'd overslept, that dawn would break soon. Considering she'd tossed and turned most of the night, it was no wonder her internal clock had gone haywire, but that was no excuse! Quickly, she leapt from the sofa, shivering in the chill. The fire had long since died out, and her panties and long T-shirt were small protection. "Adam?" she whispered, then louder, "Adam?"

There was no answer, but he wouldn't have answered if he was still asleep. Tiptoeing through the house, she hurriedly performed her morning ritual and padded to the kitchen, brushing her hair. Dodger sat on the table, watching her with absent interest as he always did, but when she opened the refrigerator, instead of jumping inside, he called "Ack!"

"Shh," she hissed. As she rummaged for the rest of the hickory bread, she noticed an empty space where three apples had been just the day before. She had planned on having them for breakfast, but Adam must have eaten them while she was bathing. The man ate like a teenager, she thought, remembering the mountains of food her brothers and cousins had devoured in her youth. Why hadn't she considered that in her shopping?

"ACK!" snorted Dodger.

She turned with a rebuke on her lips, but his impatient expression was obvious. If he had lips, they would have been pursed. Diana shrugged and walked to the table. "What?" she whispered.

Dodger stood. "Ack," he repeated, and nosed the sheet of paper that he'd been sitting on. His mission accomplished, he darted to the counter to steal the slice of bread she'd irresponsibly left there.

Frowning, she ignored her roommate's theft and read the note. "Gone hunting for fairies," it read. "Would you care to join me? Meet me in the meadow. Adam."

Unable to believe the evidence, she checked the bedroom. Adam was gone, all right. Before dawn? What was he up to?

Her first instinct was to crumple the paper into a tiny ball and throw it across the room, but she didn't. Something told her she and Adam had best have this out face-to-face. If he wasn't willing to give up in his quest for her body, she would have to make him see the futility of his actions.

She dressed quickly in her jeans and plaid workshirt, and trod the familiar path through the woods. The air grew warmer as she left her cabin behind. Soon the meadow stretched out before her, the wildflowers closed and patiently awaiting the sunlight, but it was empty of the one thing she wanted to see—the tall, raven-haired rogue with the devilish blue eyes.

"Punctuality is a virtue, you know."

Diana jumped. Adam's voice came from the edge of the forest she had just left, and she was almost afraid to turn and look. She must have rushed right past him! Her hands trembled. Now that the opportunity to shove him out of her life once and for all had actually come, her courage deserted her with a rush that was almost audible. "You could stand a few virtues," she rasped out, her gaze sweeping the meadow.

"Nah. It's more fun to be naughty."

His statement hardly calmed her, but years of fighting her faintheartedness clicked in. Swallowing her nerves, she turned slowly.

Diana gasped, and her hand flew to her mouth. Leaning a shoulder casually against a tree, Adam stood with one leg crossed over the other, the fringe of greenery between them barely visible. The first streaks of dawn brushed every inch of his naked body with pale rose, touching the tips of his hair with fire. He held one of the stolen apples. "Grab a fig leaf and let's get naked," he said with a wicked grin.

Her fingers shook, and her blood pressure skyrocketed. Adam, she realized, as *Adam*! How did always he know her weakest points? Did she have her fantasies tattooed on her forehead?

"I figured out something yesterday," he said, crunching a bite.

"What?" she managed, though her voice cracked.

"I figured out that it takes two to make love."

Before she could even think of a reply, he tossed her the apple, and she caught it reflexively. Startled, she could only gape wordlessly.

"If I've learned one thing in my life, it's that if you're convinced you'll be defeated, you will be, simple as that. You say you want to make love, yet you're not willing to let go, really let go." He shook his head. "It doesn't work that way, Eve."

Diana stared blankly at the apple, at the white against the red where Adam had taken his bite, the marks of his teeth visible on the skin. The sweet fragrance tickled her nostrils, blending with the first scents of the morning flowers and the smell of the earth.

A bottomless pit opened beneath her feet, and it grew larger by the moment. She knew she'd lied to herself by thinking she hadn't hoped for this. But if she did as he wanted, there would be no turning back, no changing her mind again. Unlike Eve, Diana had no innocence to lose; she knew exactly what consequences would result from her act. But did he?

"Why are you doing this?" she asked, her throat raw.

"Third time's a charm?"

"Please, don't give me flip remarks." She tightened her grip on the apple, her fingernails cutting into its skin. "Why are you so determined?"

He hesitated, then sighed. "Because I'm tired of acting as if this is an experiment. I'm tired of pretending things don't matter, Diana. They do. You do."

"Why?"

"For a woman who doesn't like to ask questions, you sure picked the most inopportune moment to start."

She glanced up, her confusion showing plainly on her face, and she didn't care. "Why?" she repeated.

Adam's body tensed. "If I told you I loved you, would you believe me?"

Her chest constricted, her rational mind warring with her heart. The only thing she could tell him was the truth. "No."

He smiled crookedly, laying his temple against the tree. "I didn't think so," he murmured. "Diana, don't try to figure me out. Don't let yourself agonize over explanations or stifle your body with suspicions. Stop thinking and just do! Sometimes there are no reasons."

"There are always reasons," she told him. "There have to be."

"Why, Goddess? Why try to force things into nice, logical holes when sometimes you just have to accept what *is*? You know that a rose has stamens, and chlorophyll, and derives nourishment from the steps of the food chain, but does that make it anything more, or less? Does it change the fragrance, or heal the prick from the thorn? No. It's still a rose, a rare and magical gift, and you should appreciate it as one."

She laughed mirthlessly. "What an ego! Now, you're a gift."

"Not me, Diana. I don't want to give you anything you don't already have. You have a magic in your soul, a bright, wonderful magic. But you hide it, you jinx yourself in all the ways I used to." He shrugged. "You have the opportunity to change it. Not me, *you*. Can you?"

He held himself away from her, allowing her to make the decision. If he had touched her, she knew she would have crumpled in a heap at his feet, and that *did* scare her. Somehow, the man seemed to see a place inside her that she hadn't examined in a long, long time, and though it made her tremble, she had the strangest feeling that his appearance in her life had been as inevitable as the rising sun. His determination, his gentle warmth, his courage in the face of adversity, all combined to give her exactly what she needed—and feared most. Why he didn't simply give up, she didn't know. But she was glad he hadn't. Like the dawn, or the tides, or the phases of the moon, she knew now that she wouldn't stop him even if she wanted to.

Closing her eyes tightly, she lifted the apple to her mouth.

The moment she touched her teeth to the exact spot where his had rested, heat spiraled through Adam, fire burned his loins. The chill morning air did nothing to cool his arousal; if anything, it intensified it.

She opened her eyes, and Adam groaned. Diana sent him a sultry message that quivered in the air between them like the heat of a desert afternoon. He stepped away from the tree, drawn into a maelstrom of sensation simply from her violet gaze. This was the siren beneath the ice maiden, the woman who had haunted him for months, but she was no two-dimensional picture, no product of his imagination. Confronted by reality, his goddess was more than he'd ever dreamed existed.

"I want to see you," he murmured, and for an instant the wary rabbit flickered. Then she nodded and lifted her hands, but he stopped her with a gesture. "Let me."

Anticipation swirled through him almost unbearably, twisting his gut into knots. He brushed his lips on hers in a gentle kiss, a promise of things to come, then he stepped back. He reached to her shirt and flipped open the first button. Her breasts swelled over her lacy bra, into the vee of the lapels. His fingers trembled. Swallowing hard, he undid the next, and the next, until she was exposed to her waist. Reverently, he pushed it down her shoulders.

She shivered, and her nipples pebbled against the silky fabric. Adam moaned and tugged her shirt farther, bending to slide it to her wrists. Capturing her hands behind her, he buried his face in her hair, brushed his cheek to her neck. Her spicy carnation scent rose from her skin, dizzying him. His blood coursed through him, a throbbing, pulsating flood, and he wanted to take her right there, standing. But still he held himself under control.

He released her wrists and slid his palms to her breasts, caressing the undersides as he pushed them upward. His breath came ragged in his throat, but he resisted the urge to throw her down and bury himself in her. Staying upright with an effort, he reached behind her and unclasped her bra.

Diana grabbed his shoulders as he freed her aching breasts, the pit no longer beneath her feet but inside of her. The touch of the chill air on her back was a rough counterpoint to his fingers as they returned to her hard nipples, brushing them with quick strokes that pulled at her womanhood. She gasped at the sensation that rippled through her, and tightened her grip on him. His dark head bent once more, and when his hot mouth closed over a pebbled bud, her fingernails dug into his skin.

His hands cupped her buttocks. Almost roughly, he pulled her against him, lifting her from the ground. She buried her hands in his hair, holding him to her breast. He drew her legs apart, drawing them to either side of him, pressing his hard stomach into the hot place between her thighs. His body rubbed her through her jeans, his tongue teased and suckled and tugged at the inner core of her being until it wound tighter and tighter. A moan built inside of her, caught with the swelling sensation, building until the pressure became too much for any mortal woman to fight any longer. A cry of pure delight rose in her throat, and she let it out joyfully.

As if it had been a signal, Adam groaned against her. Without releasing her, he lowered her to the ground, to the spongy bed of leaves and new grass. His body covered hers, his raven hair caressed her naked skin, his hard arousal pressed against her thigh. The suckling at her nipple intensified, his tongue swirling around and around, until again the pleasure became almost too painful to endure. Diana found herself writhing, sliding her leg against him, and he groaned again.

His mouth left her breast and moved to her neck. Vaguely, Diana wondered why, selfishly wanting that feeling to go on forever. That moment of ecstasy hadn't been enough. The pleasure swelled, crying for completion, for more than a snatch of paradise. More, she thought, she wanted more. When his hand clutched the snap of her jeans, she knew that soon the manhood she felt against the outside of her would be inside, thrusting into her, raising her to the place she'd just glimpsed . . . where souls meshed, where no secrets lived.

The rasping of the zipper sounded unnaturally loud in her ears, but she had seen the other side of the door and wanted in, no matter what the cost.

Adam felt her tense beneath him, and hesitated.

"Don't stop," she said, lifting her hips to him. "Please don't stop."

His arousal throbbed against her thigh, urging the union. Swiftly, he returned to her breasts, to knead and lick the swollen globes. "Don't think," he murmured. "Let it happen."

"I will." Her voice was breathless. "Oh, Lord, I want you, Adam." His hand slid her pants downward, and she caught it reflexively. She moaned, deep in her throat, like a tortured animal. "No!" she cried defiantly, and released him. "We will be lovers!"

For an eternal moment, Adam's whirling mind followed her line of thought, rationality overpowering hunger. "But we're already lovers," he whispered, his chest tightening with realization.

Her eyes widened. "But—"

"We're already lovers," he repeated urgently. "In every way save one, we have crossed the bounds of intimacy, and you are more than I could ever dream of. Nothing ugly is inside of you, only brightness and beauty. The cage is unlocked, Goddess, the door is open. Set yourself free."

"I—" Tears blurred her vision. Her fear, her uncertainty, made her tremble. "Adam?" Her voice was that of a child, hovering at the edge of a precipice.

His blue eyes intense with longing and knowledge, he kissed her with all the untamed passion in his soul, the undisguised yearning of a lifetime. "I love you," he murmured, then again, against her mouth, "I love you."

With a cry pulled from her soul, she flung her arms around his neck. Her lips parted beneath his, and she probed into him with her tongue, inflaming his body to a fever pitch, his mind to new bounds. Her hand dipped to his manhood, brushed away his only concealment and touched him, sliding her palm over the satin skin.

With a moan, he stripped off her pants, his own hand finding and rubbing the mound between her thighs, echoing her caress. Quickly, she left him, and her fingers dug into his buttocks, urging him over her. "I love you," she said fiercely, and pulled him to her, giving him everything within her, even as she demanded. He plunged into her hot, welcoming body, and filled her aching emptiness with the swelling fire of the beast.

Her long legs tight around him, his face buried in the sweet carpet of hair, he thrust into the endless depths of her soul, the darkness banished by the light of her love. Together they rocked in the most magical of dances, older than the hills around them, a worship of life and hope, of past and future, of love and knowledge. Faster and faster, they lifted to meet each other, hearing the roaring of their hearts and of their souls.

And when the beast flew at last, it soared to the heavens with a double cry of release and freedom.

Ten

The spring sun blanketed them with warmth as they lay intertwined on their bed of leaves. Adam held her as if she might disappear into the morning, still awed in the wake of their flight, and kissed her gently on the temple.

Diana lay in the protective circle of his arms, her naked body pressed to his as she returned to the earth she loved. But it was no longer a place of categorized quantities. It was a place of magic. The meadow shimmered with the rainbow colors of fairy lights, the wood sighed with the whispered words of sprites, and the creek, far away, chuckled with the laughter of naiads. Her trust in this man had given her something she never even realized was missing.

"Did I hurt you?" she murmured.

"Not in a million years."

"I mean when I grabbed your . . . Adam, your poor bottom. And your—"

"Will you stop worrying? I'm fine. I'm more than

fine." His voice raised to echo through the hills. "I'm in love!"

Slowly, her violet eyes brimming with joy, she lifted herself over him. "Oh, Adam," she whispered. "What have you done to me?"

He affected affront. "*Moi*? The man with the monster ego?"

She gave him a quivering smile and lightly clouted him. "You're insufferable, you know that?"

"Of course." At odds with his tone, he brushed a strand of bittersweet hair from her brow with a tenderness that made her ache. "Is it so bad, Goddess?"

She shook her head, tumbling his efforts. "It's beautiful."

He smiled and drew her down for a long, satisfying kiss. "You're beautiful."

Sighing, she returned to nestle beside him. "How did you know?"

He chuckled. "Woman, can't you even enjoy something without analyzing it to death?"

"Sorry. But no. Dammit, Adam, I didn't even know why I was jinxed." She hesitated. "To be honest, I'm still not sure."

"Diana, you were never jinxed."

"Adam—" He cut off her words with his fingertips. She bit him.

"Vixen." He stroked her mouth. "But you believed you were. I figured out that you weren't afraid of sex or even love. You are a woman obsessed with your privacy. You fought the moment of surrender because you're a born fighter, but you fought the intimacy even harder because you're terrified that your soul would be bared to someone."

"But you would never violate that," she whispered.

"Never. Because it isn't a violation. With us, it's

not a conquest or an invasion. It's a sharing." He tightened his arms around her. "For a believer in balance, you've been sadly out of kilter, Goddess."

Diana realized the truth of his words, but she knew it was more. For the first time in her life, she was truly in love.

Her eyes stung. "For a believer in luck and magic, you've done an awful lot of rational thinking."

He laughed aloud. "We're quite a pair, Goddess. I don't know how we're going to survive each other. Me, jogging through life without a road map, and you, stifling a whole other side of your nature."

Her arms tightened around him. "I love you," she whispered, and forced away a sudden shadow of doubt.

A long time later, Adam lifted his face from the sweet curve of her neck, utterly sated and complete a second time. "Am I too heavy?" he murmured.

"No." Diana sighed beneath him and raked her fingers lightly over his back. Her brows flew together suddenly, and she wriggled her fanny. "But, Adam, I itch. That isn't poison ivy we're lying on, is it?"

He shook his head. "I'm not a total novice, you know. We've just been lying in a pile of clover."

"Why haven't I noticed it until now?"

"We've been rather . . . occupied, Goddess."

"I think we should leave Eden and hustle our naked bodies back to the cabin, don't you?"

Chuckling, he raised himself to his elbows and picked a leaf from her hair. "As long as we can continue in that wonderful bed of yours."

"Of course!" Her eyes narrowed. "That reminds

me. I know the chase is over, but do I get any more fantasies? I mean, just out of curiosity."

"I don't see why not. I think I can promise you a few surprises." As his gaze flickered over her, he saw something on the ground beside her head, something long and gray and sinuous that did not belong in the bright carpet of her hair. He blinked and stared.

Two glistening eyes stared back.

He went cold all over. "Diana," he whispered.

"Don't evade the issue, Yankee."

"Don't move, honey," he croaked out.

"What's wrong?"

Mentally running through his scant knowledge of zoology, he identified the snake as nonpoisonous from the shape of its head and eyes. He didn't know what it was, but he knew what it wasn't, and though that relieved one worry, it didn't counteract the other. According to her journal, Diana was terrified of snakes.

"Sit up, honey. Very slowly."

Her eyes widened at his tone, and she turned her head. Reacting instinctively, he shot to his knees, grabbed the reptile, and flung it sideways.

"It's okay, honey," he said quickly, his body trembling in the wake of concern. "It never touched you."

Braced for her scream, he just stared when she looked at him quite calmly and said, "It was just a little garter snake, Adam. It wouldn't have hurt you."

He gaped. "But I thought—" He glanced to the sluggishly moving snake, and then back to her. His heartbeat refused to slow to normal. "You—" His mouth worked, his mind unable to form a coherent sentence.

"Are you afraid of them?" She patted his hand, sat up, and groped for her clothes. "It's all right, Adam, honest. I used to be terrified of them too, but I'm not anymore. I had to get over my fear to survive out here." She glanced over with a tiny shudder, but her voice was matter-of-fact. "The place is crawling with them, you know. We just plopped down in his space, that's all. They hibernate, just like bears. I don't know why he didn't make an appearance earlier." She stood and looked down at it. "Yuck. I don't like them very much, but they're part of the balance of nature. Are you coming?"

Adam sank back on his heels, his head bowed and shoulders shaking. "I love you, Diana Machlen," he said with a chuckle, then threw his arms wide. "And I love this crazy Eden!"

They continued exploring the boundaries of their newfound wonder well into the night. They told each other of their respective childhoods, and Diana held him tightly when he told her of the alienation he had suffered from the family he had left long ago, of the humiliation he had felt when his glorious baseball career had ended with a trade from one A-League team to another.

"The kiss of death," he assured her with a twinkle. "If it hadn't been for Max scraping me up off the street to help run the family business, I'd probably be sweeping one. With my tongue."

It was a joke, as usual, but she felt his pain as thoroughly as if it were her own.

"Hey, Goddess," he murmured, seeing her tears. "It was a great deal. Max means more to me than anything in the world." He kissed her softly. "Well, almost anything."

"I love you," she told him fiercely.

Whether snuggled deep in Diana's warm feather bed or chasing each other around the cabin, zooming in the wake of the eccentric cat, they found they could not get enough of each other. Adam, especially, was astonished to discover the ferocity of her passion. "I knew there was spice," he muttered as she ate lunch off his chest. "I never imagined such a twisted mind."

She grinned a fair imitation of his own grin, and offered him a fingerful of wild honey, which, of course, he accepted. And that set them off on a whole new tangent.

Then, while heating smoked turkey for dinner, Adam snuck up behind her to cup his palms to her naked breasts and nuzzle her neck. "It's okay," he assured her later after the turkey burned to a crisp. "Charcoal is good for the system."

"I have a one-track mind," she said. "It's a curse."

"I refuse to break this one," he murmured.

The next morning, Diana groggily lifted her head from the bed, her hair tumbled over her eyes. She winced at the bright light, then smiled and sank her face back to Adam's thigh, tickling his cheek with her foot. For the first time in three years, she'd missed her dawn excursion. And she didn't care at all. She was going to take full advantage of this bright time together.

When they finally came up for air, Adam groaned. Stiffly, he exited the bed and hobbled to the bathroom, while Diana followed, flitting around him like a butterfly. "You promised," she said with an impish smile.

He leaned into the sink, swaying. "I thought you would kill me *before* I made love to you," he said with a moan. "But I was wrong."

"C'mon, Adam. Just tell me. One little hint."

He eyed her blearily. "Don't you have something to do? Tramp through the forest? Feed the raccoons?" He yawned. "Devastate another male libido?"

"Nope."

He hung his head, chuckling weakly. "Go write about it in your journal, Goddess. Give my poor body a chance to recuperate."

She swatted the uninjured portion of his backside lightly. "I have a feeling this is a secret everybody knows."

He met her eyes in the mirror. "No, Diana. This is rare. And very, very special."

She warmed right down to her toes. "Yes, it is."

He turned to kiss her tenderly, his morning beard rasping against her cheek, then limped into the kitchen and declared that he would cook breakfast. "And then you can get us something special for dinner, O mighty hunter. I have things to do today."

Her eyes narrowed. "What things?"

"Important things." His chin lifted. "Very important things. You're not the only one with plans, you know."

A tiny smile played at the corner of his mouth. Shrugging, she backed away, but refused to keep her distance. During his preparation, she teased him, taunting him with her hands and tongue. After Dodger snuck off with the third piece of country ham, Adam frowned and rebuked her with mock sternness. She interpreted this as a challenge, one that she won.

When they'd flung open all the windows to clear away the resulting smoke from the burned eggs, Adam swept her into his arms and kissed her, walking back into the bedroom with her legs wrapped around his waist. "I wasn't hungry anyway," he murmured.

Much, much later, Adam threw a pillow at her. "Will you stop that? I want to live to a ripe old age!"

She wriggled her eyebrows. "That's too far in the future for me. I'd rather die a happy, sexually sated thirty-year-old."

"Not this time, you—you—octopus!"

"Can't handle the shoe on the other foot, huh?" she said, an air of desperation driving her.

"Yes. No." He groaned. "Diana!" When she showed no signs of relenting, he bolted from the bed and hobbled to where his jeans lay, then jerked on a green sweater. "No."

The roar of an engine outside broke into what promised to be yet another delay to the day, and Adam pulled back, chuckling. "Reality intrudes," he said, and shoved his feet into his shoes. When Diana began to do the same, he halted her quickly. "I'll go see who it is. You hold that thought."

When he limped through the door, she peeked through the open window, recognizing Matt's battered Ford pickup immediately. Adam waved and went out to meet it, leaning against the cab to talk. Matt's normally morose face actually creased in a smile once, and she echoed it, feeling her heart swell with pride. Adam could make a stone laugh, she thought.

She began to turn away, but Matt handed something to Adam, who glanced once over his shoulder at the cabin before accepting it. Frowning, she watched them for a moment longer as they shook hands, then she darted back when Adam waved good-bye.

She washed her face and pulled on her bra and panties, shivering. But whether it was from some stray chill or Adam's secretive actions, she didn't know.

"Mail call," he said gaily when he entered the cabin, then stopped, his hands on his hips. "What is that thing on your body?"

"A bra." Confused, she stared at him. "What mail?"

"Matt picked this up at Weena's, and it looked important, so he ran it by." He waved a fat envelope in the air. "Trade you for the underwear."

"Adam! That's from the university! It's the test results!"

"The rabbit died?" he asked hopefully.

She smiled at his eagerness. They had been careful, except for that first time. "That's always a possibility," she murmured, but that was for the future, and she still wasn't certain what that would hold. The present was her concern now. "This is for the tonic, you maniac."

"The dreaded dog violet!" he cried. "Bra first."

"Bra later," she said, and made a grab for the envelope, but he held it just out of her reach. Her eyes narrowed. "I'll get my shotgun."

He affected a comic expression of fear, and handed her the letter. "The last thing I need right now is another backside full of buckshot," he muttered.

"Yeah, yeah." She stared down at the envelope in her hand, a hand that suddenly trembled. Now that she had it, she wasn't sure she wanted to open it. Things had been going so well, there had to be a catch somewhere.

"So? What are you waiting for?"

"I—" She swallowed hard. "It's probably negative."

"Diana!" He embraced her, chuckling gently. "You are the oddest creature. So brash, so fiery, yet so vulnerable inside. Don't defeat yourself, love. Don't jump to one of your conclusions before all the results are in. You've been wrong before, you know. I haven't gloated over the fact that you love me." He pulled back to kiss her lightly. "Not much anyway. Open the damned thing. Make those journals of yours pay off instead of reinforcing the jinx for a change."

She snuggled into his neck, trying to dispel the shadow. "Adam? Why did you say that about my journals? What—" She swallowed hard. "Just what do you know about them?"

He tensed. "I know they're a security blanket, Goddess. I think—" He swore and held her tightly. "I don't want this to come back and haunt me later," he muttered under his breath, then braced himself, wondering if he really was crazy. "I didn't exactly tell you the whole truth about why I was originally here."

Her body stiffened. "Which is?"

"Was," he corrected firmly. "I knew your sister wanted the journal, and I owed Max. . . ."

She tried to pull away; he held her. "And so—" He paused. "I was going to steal the pages with the formula."

Taut silence reigned for two whole seconds. "You self-centered, loathsome, crawling—" Her epithets crescendoed into something approaching a roar.

Adam pinned her arms to her side, knowing he'd be dog meat if she got loose. "Listen to me! Max and I are closer than brothers, and you have an unsecured copy of the formula that can make or break him. I—" He cut himself off as she stomped on his foot and he lost his hold on her.

She threw the envelope at him. "You slimy opportunist"—She picked up the nearest object, a spoon from the table, and tossed that too—"Yankee pig!"

He leapt up to avoid it, thinking he'd really messed himself up this time, and after he'd sworn he wouldn't. "Diana, I fell in love with you!"

"I love you too, dammit! Why didn't you just ask me?"

"Would you have said yes?"

"No!"

"I knew that!" When she reached for a fork, he caught her wrist and pulled her around to face him. "I read the first entry, but I didn't steal those pages," he said urgently. "I didn't tamper with the journal, and I could have! I've had plenty of time to find the right one and walk off with it, but I couldn't even read further! Do you understand? I couldn't do it."

His words penetrated through Diana's haze of anger. Not "didn't," but "couldn't." "Why?" she asked stiffly.

"Because I realized how important they were to you." He gentled his hold slightly and pushed her hair away from her defiant violet eyes. "Because I met a woman who showed me that dreams really could come true, that I could have everything I've ever wanted. *Everything.* Not by simply wishing it true, but by making it happen." He lifted a crooked smile. "I came to steal your copy of the formula, Goddess. But you stole my heart instead."

She tried to tell herself that she was immune to charm, that she should kick him out on his lead-scarred backside once and for all. But she couldn't.

He melted her soul. "I moved it anyway," she whispered.

"You what?" He began to chuckle. "You mean I looked in the cabinet—"

"And it was never there." A giggle bubbled from her throat. "I hid it after Emma called."

"Oh, Diana." He hugged her and lifted her from her feet. "You are a constant surprise to me, you know that?"

She returned his embrace and pressed her mouth to his. "I love you," she whispered, almost desperately.

"I love you too, Goddess." He set her gently on the floor and grinned his jaunty grin. "Do you know what we should do? We should pull that dumb thing out and burn it. It's caused enough problems already."

Her throat tightened. "Adam—"

His smile faded. "I'm pushing, aren't I? I'm sorry, Goddess. Erase that." He swept the air with his hands. "We have too much going for us. I still have a few things up my sleeve, and like any true believer in magic, I'm not going to mess it up. We have a lot to look forward to."

She wanted to believe him. "Like another fantasy?" she asked breathlessly.

He rolled his eyes, then gently shoved her away. "You'll get your fantasy, Goddess. Maybe even more surprises than you can handle. Just give me time. Now, open that envelope!"

She'd almost forgotten the analysis. She picked up the letter, weighed it in her palm, then took a deep breath. "Okay, here goes." She ripped the seal and yanked out the computer printouts. She read the first page and frowned, then went to the next, letting the excess tumble to the floor.

Adam glanced at them. "Gibberish," he muttered.

"No, not gibberish, tincture and spectro—" She gasped and pointed. "Adam, look!"

He echoed her gasp playfully. "It's a fingernail! Oh, Diana, I'm so happy for you!"

She smiled. "I was right," she said in wonder. "Dammit, Adam, it was that dog violet!"

"See? Everything's going to be great!"

She hugged him fiercely, almost believing it herself. "But I still have a lot of work to do on the paper," she told him.

"Always finding the dark cloud in your silver lining, huh?" He blew a tolerant sigh, released her, and turned her toward the stillroom. "Well, what are you waiting for? Win that Nobel!"

"Adam!" She squirmed, hating herself for her doubts. "I think it can wait until tomorrow."

"No, you go to it. Nose to the grindstone, the whole bit. I'll manage."

He looked so woebegone, she giggled. "You're terrible."

"I know. Actually, I really do have some loose ends to take care of."

Diana watched his escape, telling herself she had nothing to worry about. "Chicken!"

He clucked madly. "Go pick some plantain or something!" He grinned and kissed her nose. "Don't forget to close the windows. And make sure those journals are safe," he told her in mock sternness as he backed out the door. "Remember, we have a date in Vienna."

"Stockholm!"

"Whatever!"

Moments later, his Porsche roared away.

Diana smiled gently and finished dressing, anticipation for her next fantasy quivering through her. Lost in her thoughts, she put her shirt on inside out, swore, then reversed it, and slid her arms into the sleeves.

With half the buttons done up, she froze. A shiver played over her spine as she remembered another superstition, one that said that if you put on a garment wrong side out, bad luck would follow unless you wore it that way all day.

"Nonsense," she said, and finished her task. "I'd look ridiculous!" A chill breeze seemed to sweep through her, and she bolted out the door without a backward glance.

Diana hurried through her gathering, a vague feeling of unease plaguing her despite her best efforts. Crockett and his mate chittered somewhere nearby, but for the first time in years she felt no need to follow. Something told her to get home.

When she approached the cabin from the side, the silence struck her first. Like a woodland creature sensing danger, she stopped, tilting her head up to search her surroundings. Adam's Porsche was still gone from beside her Jeep, but otherwise she could detect no problem. Wondering what had alerted her, she set her basket down carefully and eased around to the front. The door was closed.

She frowned, then shook herself sternly. Dammit, now was not the time to question her good fortune or see shadows in her happiness. She was in love, Adam loved her, and everything would be fine. It was only that stupid omen that made her so suspicious, she thought, and pushed the door open.

She halted, frozen by the sight which met her eyes. Bunches of dried herbs from her stillroom had been tossed all over furniture. The flour container was dumped on the counter, its contents scattered. A chair lay overturned. The refrigerator door stood open; milk dripped from the shelf to puddle on the floor. It looked as if someone had searched the cabin in a hurry, uncaring of the consequences.

The blood left her face in a rush. She picked up a piece of broken pottery, the remains of the Corsican mint, and her hands trembled as she remembered Adam's confession. Having everything, huh? Loose ends, huh? Had he decided to find the final journal? Had her jinx had the last laugh after all?

Tears blurred her eyes, her nostrils flared. "Damn," she whispered. "Damn, damn, damn!"

Eleven

Adam whistled something happy and tuneless and completely nonsensical as he bounded down the road, his hands shoved deeply into his jacket pockets. The air around him was warm. Spring had indeed come to Diana's shadowed ridge, and it would never again be winter—not if he had anything to say about it.

His fingers brushed over the paper inside, and his grin widened. His final surprise was signed, sealed, and delivered, and he hoped it would be her ultimate fantasy. He knew it was his. Though it had taken the sale of his precious Porsche, he didn't care anymore. He had Diana, he had a place he belonged, and he had a future. His dreams could finally come true. All of them.

The cabin loomed up ahead. The door and several of the windows stood open. Giving an exuberant holler, he took the embankment in a headlong rush. "Hey!" he cried as he ran across the clearing. "Oh, June, I'm home!"

Diana walked onto the porch, her red hair dancing around her shoulders, but her violet eyes didn't fill with the love he'd expected, her arms didn't open wide. In fact, her gaze chilled him. And her hands were quite encumbered.

Diana lifted her shotgun and aimed it carefully. At him.

Adam halted mere feet from the porch, gaping at her. Unwilling to believe the evidence, he blinked and looked again. Twin barrels still stared back. "Is it a battle, Santa Ana?" he asked, his heart pounding.

"It never stopped," she said.

"Would you mind telling me what's going on?" He'd meant to ask the question calmly, but his voice rose to something like a roar. "And what in the hell are you doing with that thing?"

"My cabin is trashed, Yankee, but I think you already know that."

"I don't know what you're talking about!" He closed his eyes, fighting for control. "Goddess, calm down. Whatever has happened, we can work it out."

"Stop it. It won't work this time. You can't charm your way out of this."

He tensed. "Out of what?"

The barrel wavered. "You couldn't leave it alone, could you? You couldn't let my journals rest. You had to go ahead and try to find it, didn't you?"

"The what?" His temper snapped with an almost audible crack. "No!" Without thinking twice, he rushed toward her and grabbed the gun.

"Stop it, damn you!" she cried. "Everything's ruined!"

The blood roared in his ears as he broke the gun open and ejected the shells, then flung it far from them. With a snarl, he whirled back to her and snatched her shoulders. "Listen to me! I didn't touch your journals or your cabin! I wouldn't hurt you! I love you!"

She shook him off, tears of defiance pooling in her eyes. 'It won't work, Adam. Just leave me alone!"

She spun away and ran into the cabin. Adam reached out to snag her sleeve, but he missed. He chased her inside, fury coursing through him.

Over the threshold, he paused, looking around at the chaos, then stomped after Diana, who had bolted to the stillroom. She stood before the cabinet, her hands pressed together.

"It's still locked, isn't it?" he asked tightly.

She nodded, her shoulders rigid. "I told you it's not there."

His chest heaved in indignation. "So you think I tried to find it elsewhere."

She said nothing.

"Great," he muttered, and returned to the main room, searching for proof. "You left the windows open," he told her, then looked for more. Flour trailed over the counter, and in the white powder he found what he wanted. "Diana?" he called tersely. "Come here."

"No."

"Now!"

She edged into the room, her eyes wide and suspicious. "What?"

He pointed. "Footprints, Diana. Raccoon footprints!"

She looked, then glanced up at him. "Oh," she whispered, her voice trembling. "But you disappeared, and—and after what you said this morning, I thought—"

"What? That your jinx finally kicked in again?"

At her hesitant nod, his jaw clenched. Something inside him went icy cold. "Thanks for your trust, Goddess. I really appreciate it."

"Adam, I'm sorry." Her lip trembled. "I just thought everything was too good to be true, and . . ." She trailed off with a ragged sigh.

"And so you did your usual conclusion jump and came up with a nice *logical* solution." That hurt him more than a shotgun blast ever could.

She nodded again, her hand reaching to him tentatively. "I'm sorry, Adam."

He flinched away, unable to warm the chill in his soul. "Where's Dodger?"

"I don't know, he—"

"Dodger?" he called softly, making enticing little noises with his lips. When he heard a distant snort, he went toward the door, his steps heavy. "He's under the porch. Amazing how your compassion flies out the window when your little magic shield is threatened, isn't it?"

"Adam!" she cried, but he didn't stop. "Dammit, come back here!"

Diana righted the overturned chair with a thump, fighting tears. Why didn't he say something? Why did he just stare at her, his blue eyes so hard? Couldn't he see she was trying to apologize?

He returned, cradling the shivering Dodger in his hands. "He's not injured," Adam said coldly. "He's only scared. But I guess you know all about that, huh?"

She braced herself, crossing her arms in front of her. "No, I wouldn't. Maybe this time it was raccoons, but what about next time?"

"And you are absolutely convinced there will be a next time, aren't you?"

"Just say it, Adam."

"What?"

"That you're leaving me."

His eyes grew colder. "You'd like that, wouldn't you?"

"No." She met his gaze, the very air crackling between them. It lasted so long, she began to tremble with the strain. "Say something," she muttered. "I don't even recognize you."

"Good," he said. "It's about time you thought of someone besides yourself."

Her chest heaved. "Me! How dare you! You never had any intention of staying here!"

"How would you know? You never asked."

"I'm sure you would have said exactly the right thing! You were all over me from day one, and oh-so-wonderful and flippant. But I was just a roll in the hay, Adam, right? A bit more trouble than most, but that made the challenge greater. Why don't you admit it and get it over with!"

She glared at him; he stared back.

"Just my luck," he said with a grim smile. "I fell in love with the one woman in the world who makes things go wrong."

Her lip trembled. "I don't do it purposely. I hate this!"

"No, you don't, Diana. You love that jinx."

She gasped. "Adam!"

He nodded. "You slam that damned door every time, don't you? You're like Dodger, you know. You keep trying to escape, but you just entrench yourself beneath the porch. You trade one cage for another, and you love it. It's a nice, safe place to hide, and you need that security." He waved one hand around. "Out here, everything is predictable, isn't it? The seasons, the plants, the animals. Out here, the more you know, the safer you are. You won't eat something poisonous, you won't try to pick up a deadly snake, or accidentally stumble into a bear's den. And that jinx is so predictable, such an easy excuse. 'Sorry, I don't have a headache, but *you* will if you touch me. I can't help myself.' But people won't stay safely tucked away into their little cubbyholes, and that scares the hell out of you."

"No!"

"You set your world on the diagonal, you spice up your life with every bite you take. You believe in magic, Goddess, in surprises, but you keep snuggling back down in that cage." He stared at her another moment then he turned away. "This time I won't let you."

Slowly, deliberately, he moved around the cabin, closing the windows. He set Dodger carefully beside the puddle of milk and shut the refrigerator. "Where are your keys?" he asked quietly.

"Where's your baby? What's the matter, couldn't your car—"

"Where are your damned keys!"

His controlled bellow made her swallow hard. "In my jacket," she said in a small voice. "There on the chair."

He took them from her pocket with not so much as a jingle. Then he turned on her and advanced.

Seeing the fury on his face, Diana shrank back from him. A part of her gaped in awe at the intensity of his temper, but she still flinched when his hand darted out to snatch hers. Before she could say a word, he dragged her out the door and tossed her into the Jeep.

"I don't owe you an explanation," he said, the muscle in his jaw working. "But I'm going to give you one anyway."

He didn't speak again. The engine roared to life, and he slammed it into gear and spit dirt in his exit. He drove straight up the embankment and whirled onto the road. When they reached the first turn, he took it at a speed that made her head bash against the door. She grabbed the safety bar and held on for dear life.

"Where are we going?" she asked, clutching the bar as he swerved to miss a rabbit.

"You're so good at conclusions, you figure it out."

She bit her lip and stared through the windshield. The trip seemed endless, but when they pulled up before Matt's lodge, she knew it could only have taken minutes. "Why are we here?" she asked, considerably subdued.

He gave her an unreadable look. "Get out."

She scrambled for the exit. Adam strode ahead of her. She hurried to follow. At the carved door, he paused long enough to remove his keys from his jeans, and inserted one into the lock. He pushed it open with a flourish and turned back to her. "Surprise," he said with no emotion whatsoever.

Inside, before the great gaping maw of the fireplace, lay a flowing nest of black fabric, the coverings from the furniture. Two glasses of wine rested on the hearth. Her throat tightened. "You bought it," she whispered.

It wasn't a question, but he answered it anyway with a nod. "I figured that with your unusual wild recipes and my know-how to sell the place to the rich and exclusive, we could make one hell of a future together. I had it all planned out." He snorted mirthlessly and closed the door softly. "As usual, things got a little screwed up."

"Adam—" she began, but the tears that suddenly stung her eyes crowded the words right out.

"It's really quite amusing, isn't it?" he asked. "I thought I finally had it all." After a cold look at her, he turned and loped away. "You don't need a jinx, you know. You do just fine all by yourself."

"Where are you going?"

"Weena's. I had Emma send the rest of my stuff there."

"But . . ." Her breath caught. "You're still keeping the place?"

"Yeah. Some things are worth fighting for." He paused and glanced over his shoulder. "Aren't they, Diana?"

He didn't stop long enough to hear her answer. Shoving his hands deep into his pockets, he kicked a rock from his path and kept walking.

Diana numbly watched him recede down the road, silent tears spilling down her cheeks. She deserved his contempt. She had hurt him, wounded more than his body. Her mistrust had stabbed deeper than any physical blow, and her heart ached for him.

She leaned back against the door, holding herself tightly as her unseeing gaze wandered over the grazing horses, the distant shadowed hills. Her first instinct was to turn and run, but she couldn't. Though he hadn't said the word "coward," he should have. From the very first day, she'd been an absolute shrew, shoving him away with her anger and fear, as she had with everybody all of her life. Yet he'd always laughed her off, not because he was a masochist, but because he had a special brand of courage that she admired.

Sighing raggedly, she realized she loved his humor more than anything else about him.

A hysterical giggle bubbled to the surface as she finally figured out the secret of his magic. But was it too late to prove to him that what they had was worth fighting for?

She wiped her tears away and turned to the door. Tentatively, she tried the handle, and found it unlocked. Her gaze flew to the horses, and an idea began to form.

Adam shoved his hands deep into his jeans pockets, hunching his shoulders. The twilight cry of a whippoorwill echoed the emptiness in his heart. The miles between the lodge and the cottage had never seemed so long as they did now, the stretch of road so lonely. He stepped over a rock, unable to draw up his anger to kick it, unable even to wince as the movement pulled his injury. Nothing in his life compared to this, he thought. He was absolutely numb, inside and out.

He started and froze as a rabbit bolted from the undergrowth and darted into his path. It halted, eyeing him, its nose twitching. Hesitantly, it inched toward him, then stopped and dashed away.

To his surprise, he almost found a smile for the creature, and he knew he wasn't as numb as he'd thought. Deep within him, foolishly perhaps, burned a spark of hope. Diana Machlen had only begun to spread her wings, to explore the world outside her cover. With time and patience, she would stop using her jinx against him. He just couldn't do it by himself anymore. She had opened up to him, and he breathed a silent prayer that she would again.

His steps somewhat lighter, he eyed the long miles still ahead and glanced up at a sky the color of Diana's eyes. "Nice dramatic gesture," he muttered. "I should have taken the Jeep."

As he trudged on, a strange pounding noise sounded, as if from the earth itself. Frowning, he looked back at the clear sky, then around him, but could not find the source. One of Weena's gorier tales, of a phantom stallion searching for its master at any cost, haunted him briefly, but he shook that off and continued walking.

It grew louder, and definitely came from behind him. He spun, and the heart that had been so empty brimmed with sudden, incredible joy.

A white horse galloped madly toward him. And on its back, a vision in a flowing black cape, clung Diana.

"Stand and deliver!" she shouted.

Adam froze, wondering if his heart would burst with love for her.

The bandit raced closer, gripping the pommel. Her bittersweet hair streamed behind her, confined only by another strip of black tied at her temples. He could see her beautiful mouth set in grim determination. "Oh, Goddess," he whispered, swallowing a lump in his throat.

"Stand and deliver," she repeated, but her words ended in a shriek as she overshot him. With a curse, she turned the horse in a wide arc, crunching through the undergrowth as she growled disparaging comments on the steed's parentage.

Adam tried to contain his laughter but couldn't. "Show him who's boss!" he cried, his voice quivering. "Your victim awaits!"

"You can hee-haw all you want, Yankee! You just wait until you're up here too!" Her turn complete, she urged the horse to him at a sedate walk. She drew up beside him, looked down at him for a moment, then dropped her gaze and fidgeted with the reins.

Adam's smile gentled, recognizing the awkward signs. "Hi," he said.

"This isn't how it was supposed to go," she muttered. "I was going to sweep you off your feet and carry you off into the sunset. But I—" She cleared her throat and met his gaze suddenly. Her eyes glittered behind the mask. "I'm so sorry, Adam. All my life, I've faced my fears, but I really messed up this time. Because instead, I caused it. I hurt you, and that was my biggest fear of all. You've taken more abuse from me than I deserve. I've been a real—"

"Don't say it, Goddess." Before she could comment, he swung up behind her, gritting his teeth as his backside hit the saddle. "Just ravish me."

She swiveled her head around and blinked. "You don't want the long, drawn-out version?"

He shook his head and kissed her stubborn mouth. "I love you," he whispered. "And you made the first move. A grand, magical, fantastical first move."

Her lip quivered. "I love you so much. I—" She snuggled against him and clicked her tongue. The horse started back toward the lodge at a lope. "I don't want a security blanket, Adam. I want to be with you, and I do believe in magic. At least between us. I'll try and control my temper, I promise."

"Don't," he murmured in her ear. "It adds the spice to the sweetness, Goddess. It always has." He bit her lobe lightly. "You're a passionate woman in everything. I don't want to change that."

She moaned, and her legs tightened. Taking that as a command, the horse picked up the pace, first to a trot, then a full-blown gallop.

Adam winced as he bounced. "Why is this always so romantic in the movies?" he cried. "How can anyone possibly get excited when their bones are being ground into dust?"

"I don't know! Just hang on tight. I'm not sure I can steer this thing!"

"This does not comfort me!"

"I'm sorry! I should have taken the Jeep!"

"I love you!" He spit out her hair as it filled his mouth, and laughed his happiness to the wind.

The rosy dawn streaked over the horizon, touching them as they snuggled together, leaning against Diana's Jeep. "It's really ours?" she whispered, awed by the magic of the night, the sunrise, and the man holding her. "It's not going to disappear with the morning?"

"We have it all, Goddess. Now and forever."

She kissed him lingeringly, then drew back and held her ear to his heart. "I believe it," she murmured. "But I have one question."

"Hmm?"

"How did you know about the fantasies?" Not her journals, she knew, she'd believed him when he'd said he'd read only one entry.

He chuckled, a deep, reverberating sound that made her tremble to her toes. He reached into his jacket pocket without releasing her and drew out a folded scrap of paper. "I had a little help."

She opened it, and her eyes widened. "That's me!" she said. "The portrait!"

He nodded, his arms tightening.

"But Adam, the sheikh, the Roman . . . They're not here. None of them."

He shrugged. "I guessed," he told her smugly.

No, she thought. He knew. He always knew. But she wouldn't let him gloat about it. Grinning, she peeked up at him. "Did you know twins run in my family?"

"Twins?" His heartbeat accelerated against her cheek. "Really?"

She twined her arms around his neck and nodded firmly. "Runs in the family," she whispered against his mouth.

An odd hissing sound filled the air around them.

"Adam?" she asked, nibbling on his lips. "What are the odds of all four of the tires going flat at the same time?"

He shushed her in the most magical way possible.

And her spirits soared.

THE EDITOR'S CORNER

May is a special month here at LOVESWEPT. It's our anniversary month! We began publishing LOVESWEPTs in May 1983, and with your encouragement and support we've been at it ever since. One of the hallmarks of the LOVESWEPT line has always been our focus on our authors. The six authors whose books you can look forward to next month represent what we feel is the true strength of our line—a blend of your favorite tried-and-true authors along with several talented newcomers. The books these wonderful writers have penned just for you are as unique and different as the ladies themselves.

Helen Mittermeyer leads off the month with the second book in her *Men of Ice* trilogy, **BLACK FROST**, LOVESWEPT #396. Helen's legions of fans often remark on the intensity of emotion between her characters and the heightened sense of drama in her novels. She won't disappoint you at all with **BLACK FROST!** Hero Bear Kenmore, a race-car driver with nerves of steel, gets the thrill of his life when he meets heroine Kip Noble. Bear has never met a woman whose courage and daring equals his own, but Kip is his match in every way. For Kip, falling in love with Bear is like jumping into an inferno. She's irrevocably drawn to him yet has to struggle to keep her independence. Helen has once again created characters who barely keep from spontaneously combusting when they're together. Helen's "men of ice" are anything but!

Jan Hudson's latest treat is **STEP INTO MY PARLOR**, LOVESWEPT #397. With three previous books to her credit, this sassy Texas lady has captured your attention and doesn't plan to let it go! She brings characters to life who are true to themselves in every way and as straightforward as Jan herself. You'll enjoy the ride as her unabashedly virile hero, Spider Webb, falls hard for lovely socialite Anne Foxworth Jennings. Anne is out of cash and nearly out of hope when she meets the seductive pirate, Spider. He almost makes her forget she has to stay one step ahead of the man who'd threatened her life. But in Spider's arms she's spellbound, left breathless with yearning. Caught in his tender web, Anne discovers that she no longer fears for her life because Spider has captured her soul. **STEP INTO MY PARLOR** will grab you from page one!

Joan Elliott Pickart's **WHISPERED WISHES**, LOVESWEPT
(continued)

#398, tells the love story of Amnity Ames and Tander Ellis. You may remember Tander as the sexy computer expert friend of the hero from **MIXED SIGNALS,** #386. Joan just had to give Tander his due, and he falls for Amnity like a rock! Can you imagine a gorgeous hunk walking into a crafts store and telling the saleswoman he's decided to take up needlepoint! Tander does just that and Amnity never suspects he's got ulterior motives—she's too busy trying to catch her breath. Joan's characters always testify to the fact that there is a magical thing called love at first sight. Her books help renew your spirit and gladden your heart. You won't be able to resist feeling an emotional tug when Amnity whispers her wishes to Tander. Enjoy this special story!

One of the newcomers to LOVESWEPT is Terry Lawrence— an author we think has an exciting future ahead of her. You may have read Terry's first LOVESWEPT, **WHERE THERE'S SMOKE, THERE'S FIRE,** which was published in the fall of 1988. Since then, Terry has been hard at work and next month her second book for us hits the shelves, **THE OUTSIDER,** LOVESWEPT #399. Both the hero and the heroine of this sensually charged romance know what it's like to be outsiders, and in each other's arms they discover what it feels like to belong. When Joe Bond catches Susannah Moran switching dice in the casino he manages in his Ottawa Indian community, he has to admit the lady is good— and temptingly beautiful. Just doing her job investigating the casino's practices, Susannah has to admit she's never been caught so fast and never by a man who set off alarms all over her body! These two special people don't find it easy to bridge the differences between their cultures. But what does come easily is the overwhelming need and desire they feel for each other. Terry will surely win loads of new readers with this tender, evocatively written love story. You'll want to count yourself among them!

We published Patt Bucheister's very first LOVESWEPT, **NIGHT AND DAY,** back in early 1986, and what a smash debut it was! Now, many books and many fans later, Patt presents you with another delicious delight, **THE ROGUE,** LOVESWEPT #400. A warm and generous lady with a sunny disposition, Patt naturally creates such a heroine in Meredith Claryon. When Meredith receives a strange phone call one night from a man demanding she answer his ques-

(continued)

tions, Meredith handles the situation with her usual grace and aplomb. Paul Rouchett is so intrigued by the lady he's never met that he decides he has no choice but to convince her to team up with him to find the embezzler who'd robbed his nightclub and run off with her sister. And what a team they make! The tart-tongued nurse and the owner of the Rogue's Den are an unbeatable duo—but discovering that for themselves leads them on a merry, romantic chase. Patt's strong belief in love and romance couldn't come across better than in this well-crafted book.

Have you every wondered exactly what makes a guy a good ol' boy? Having lived my entire life north of the Mason-Dixon line, I can tell you I have! But after reading **LOVIN' A GOOD OL' BOY** by Mary Kay McComas, LOVESWEPT #401, I wonder no more. Hero Buck LaSalle is a good ol' boy in the flesh, and when Yankee Anne Hunnicut hits town in her high heels and designer suits, Buck leaves no doubt in her mind about the term. He has the sexiest smile she's ever seen and too much charm for his own good, and although he's none too pleased about why she's there, he shows her in more ways than she ever imagined how much he wants her to stay. With her inimitable style, Mary Kay will have you giggling or sighing with pleasure or shedding a tear—probably all three—before you finish this sure-to-please romance. You'll long for a good ol' boy of your own.

Since we like to set the books in our anniversary month apart, we're going to surprise you with our cover design next month. But you're used to surprises from us, right? It makes life more interesting—and fun!

All best wishes.

Sincerely,

Susann Brailey

Susann Brailey
Editor
LOVESWEPT
Bantam Books
666 Fifth Avenue
New York, NY 10103

FAN OF THE MONTH

Jane Calleja

It was the colorful cover which prompted me to buy my first LOVESWEPT. I was already an avid reader of romance books then, but the unique stories and interesting characters in the LOVESWEPTs brought new meaning to romance for me.

New issues arrived here in the Philippines each month featuring original and delightful plots. I fell in love with the heroes and heroines of Barbara Boswell, Iris Johansen, Fayrene Preston, Joan Elliott Pickart, Kay Hooper, and Sandra Brown. The authors were able to capture everyday human emotions and make their characters come alive. I would like to thank these writers for answering my letters despite their hectic schedules.

My wish is to be able to join the ranks of the LOVESWEPT authors in the future. Right now I am nineteen years old and a third-year college student. I love reading LOVESWEPTs so much that I read the same books over and over again. In fact, I've read **FOR THE LOVE OF SAMI** by Fayrene Preston more than ten times, and I plan to read it again soon. Once I start to read, I really lose track of time and place. My family just watches me queerly if I suddenly giggle or cry in the middle of reading a book. That's how vivid LOVESWEPTs are! You can't help but feel what the characters are feeling.

I was surprised, but honored and delighted to be chosen a Fan of the Month. Thank you!

60 Minutes to a Better, More Beautiful You!

Now it's easier than ever to awaken your sensuality, stay slim forever—even make yourself irresistible. With Bantam's bestselling subliminal audio tapes, you're only 60 minutes away from a better, more beautiful you!

_ 45004-2	**Slim Forever**	$8.95
_ 45112-X	**Awaken Your Sensuality**	$7.95
_ 45081-6	**You're Irresistible**	$7.95
_ 45035-2	**Stop Smoking Forever**	$8.95
_ 45130-8	**Develop Your Intuition**	$7.95
_ 45022-0	**Positively Change Your Life**	$8.95
_ 45154-5	**Get What You Want**	$7.95
_ 45041-7	**Stress Free Forever**	$7.95
_ 45106-5	**Get a Good Night's Sleep**	$7.95
_ 45094-8	**Improve Your Concentration**	$7.95
_ 45172-3	**Develop A Perfect Memory**	$8.95

THE DELANEY DYNASTY

THE SHAMROCK TRINITY

☐ 21975 RAFE, THE MAVERICK
by Kay Hooper $2.95

☐ 21976 YORK, THE RENEGADE
by Iris Johansen $2.95

☐ 21977 BURKE, THE KINGPIN
by Fayrene Preston $2.95

THE DELANEYS OF KILLAROO

☐ 21872 ADELAIDE, THE ENCHANTRESS
by Kay Hooper $2.75

☐ 21873 MATILDA, THE ADVENTURESS
by Iris Johansen $2.75

☐ 21874 SYDNEY, THE TEMPTRESS
by Fayrene Preston $2.75

THE DELANEYS: *The Untamed Years*

☐ 21899 GOLDEN FLAMES *by Kay Hooper* $3.50
☐ 21898 WILD SILVER *by Iris Johansen* $3.50
☐ 21897 COPPER FIRE *by Fayrene Preston* $3.50

THE DELANEYS II

☐ 21978 SATIN ICE *by Iris Johansen* $3.50
☐ 21979 SILKEN THUNDER *by Fayrene Preston* $3.50
☐ 21980 VELVET LIGHTNING *by Kay Hooper* $3.50